Addie McCormick

AND THE
CHICAGO SURPRISE

Leanne Lucas

HARVEST HOUSE PUBLISHERS
Eugene, Oregon 97402

Addie McCormick and the Chicago Surprise

Copyright © 1993 by Leanne Lucas
Published by Harvest House Publishers
Eugene, Oregon 97402

Library of Congress Cataloging-in-Publication Data

Lucas, Leanne, 1955–
    Addie McCormick and the Chicago surprise / Leanne Lucas.
      p. cm. — (Addie McCormick adventures ; bk. #4)
    Summary: During a visit to Chicago with their friend Miss T., Addie
and Nick find a mystery of disappearing belongings leading them to a
poor boy and a recognition of the blessings God has given them.
    ISBN 1-56507-082-8
    [1. Mystery and detective stories. 2. Christian life—
Fiction. 3. Homeless persons—Fiction. 4. Chicago (Ill.)—Fiction.]
I. Title.   II. Series: Addie McCormick and the Chicago surprise.
III. Series: Lucas, Leanne, 1955– Addie adventure series ; bk. 4.
PZ7.L96963Ab   1993
[Fic]—dc20   92-25920
                                                        CIP
                                                        AC

Printed in the United States of America.

CHAPTER 1

Operation Merry Christmas!

Addie tucked her long, black braid inside her stocking cap and pulled her gloves on. "See you at five, Dad," she said and gave her father a quick kiss on the cheek.

"All right, kiddo," he answered. "Have fun."

"Thanks for the ride, Mr. McCormick," said Nick Brady. Nick was a neighbor and a good friend of Addie's. He flipped the hood of his snowsuit up over his head and opened the back door of the car.

"Yeah, thanks," Brian Dennison echoed. Brian was another friend. He was spending the first semester of school with Nick's family because his father was opening a franchise for his company in Japan.

The three children stood ankle deep in snow and looked with delight at the scene before them. The previous night's snowfall had blanketed the ground with four inches of white powder and here, at Miss T.'s house, no one had disturbed the winter wonderland in their elderly friend's backyard. It was the perfect way to start the first day of Christmas vacation.

Addie turned around and flopped onto her back and began making snow angels. She didn't stay there long. A heavy, wet snowball plopped onto the ground next to her and Nick stood over her, holding an even larger one directly over her face. She rolled to the side just as he dropped it, then gave his pant leg a hard jerk and he fell in the snow next to her.

That started an all-out snowball war, and soon the three of them were covered with snow and red-faced from the cold.

"Time out," Brian finally gasped. He pulled his woolen cap from his head and brushed icicles out of the straight dark blond hair that fell across his forehead.

Nick slapped his hands together hard to knock off some of the snow that had caked on his gloves. Addie buried her face in the crook of her arm, trying to warm up her already cold nose.

The back door opened and Miss T. smiled at the three breathless children. "I've been watching you from the window," she laughed, "and it looks like you're getting the worst of it, Mr. Brady!"

"Oh, yeah?" Nick shouted. He scooped a handful of snow off the ground and tossed it at Miss T. He wasn't aiming to hit her, but she pulled the door shut just in case. The snow smacked harmlessly on the side of the house.

That slight vibration caused a small avalanche off the roof and several large chunks of snow powdered the steps to the back porch. Miss T. opened the door once more.

"Oh, no," Brian groaned.

"What is it?" the elderly woman asked.

He pointed silently to the road. About a quarter-mile away, they could all see the now-familiar sight of another television van approaching the house.

Nick heaved a disgusted sigh. "Company," he said to Miss T.

"Another one?" she asked in dismay. "I'm sure I don't have any appointments today."

"Since when do these guys think they need an appointment?" Nick muttered. Nick was referring to the multitude of television, newspaper, and magazine reporters who had been flocking to Miss T.'s house for the last six weeks.

Until last summer, Miss T. had simply been a little old lady living her life out in the family home in the farm country of central Illinois. But then she met Addie and Nick, and it wasn't long before the children discovered things about Miss T. no one else knew.

Forty-five years earlier, Eunice Tisdale, "Miss T." to the children, went to Hollywood seeking fame and fortune. To her surprise, she found it. She was what they called an "overnight success." The movie moguls changed her name to Tierny Bryce, and soon she was starring in films opposite Hollywood's hottest leading man, Winston Rinehart. But Tierny Bryce found she was very unhappy with the Hollywood lifestyle. Late one October evening, she had the unexpected opportunity to fake her own death and get out of Hollywood for good, and she took it. Eunice Tisdale came home to stay and she lived happily and quietly for many years.

Then came Addie and Nick, and soon her secret was out. In many ways, Miss T. was grateful the children had discovered her past. It lifted the burden of secrecy she'd carried for many years. But the price was fame, and sometimes it seemed as if there were no end to the reporters and interviews and questions. Like today.

"I suppose I'll have to talk to them," the elderly woman sighed.

"Just tell 'em to get lost," Nick suggested.

Miss T. smiled at the boy's bluntness. "I'm afraid I have to be a little more tactful than that," she said. "Although I do wish there was a polite way to discourage them."

The van pulled into the drive and around the back of the house where the three children stood. The back door slid open and the customary grunt with all the equipment hanging off his shoulders stepped out first. Then came the man with the camcorder, and finally, the reporter.

She was another pretty, perky brunette with big white teeth. Addie couldn't tell the difference between these reporters anymore, and Nick echoed her unspoken thoughts.

"Info-babe," he whispered, and Brian and Addie both grinned. Nick and his father had started calling all the young women reporters "info-babes," even though Mrs. Brady thought it was sexist and got mad if she heard them say it.

"Hi, there!" the woman said with a bright smile. "I'll bet you're Addie McCormick and Nick Brady, aren't you? That curious little boy and girl who discovered our long-lost movie star. Stick around, will you? I want to talk with you!"

Nick made a growling sound that only Addie and Brian could hear. Addie choked back her laughter and shook her head. "Our folks won't let us give interviews," she managed to say.

"Oh, just a couple of little questions?"

"I'm afraid not," Miss T. said firmly. "I must insist that you give my friends their privacy. I've promised their parents I wouldn't allow the media to grill them."

"All right, Miss Bryce," the young woman said with a saccharine smile. "I'm happy to abide by your wishes. My name is Tawny Pierson-Smythe and I'm with channel WBAB out of Chicago. Of course you won't mind if I ask *you*..."

While the reporter made the usual pitch for an interview, Nick motioned to his two friends. "Come here a second," he whispered and led them around the corner of the house. He began making fat snowballs. "Commence Operation... Merry Christmas!" he said with a fake, Tawny Pierson-Smythe grin. He threw a snowball hard and fast at the north side of the house. Brian laughed out loud and joined him.

"What in the world are you two doing?" Addie asked.

"Just help us," Nick said. "You'll understand soon enough."

"Okay," Addie said and scooped up a handful of snow. She pitched it at the house and it hit with a resounding thud.

"Good," Nick said. "Keep it up."

So Addie kept it up, and for the next minute or so snowballs hit the house with pounding regularity. Then Nick signalled for them to stop.

"Listen," he said.

They heard the brittle crack of snow shifting and they all peered around the side of the house in time to see another mini avalanche slide off the roof and onto the unsuspecting Tawny and her companions.

"Oh, my," they heard Miss T. say from inside the safety of her kitchen door. "How unfortunate! You're absolutely soaked."

Ms. Pierson-Smythe was covered in white powdery snow and the poofy brown hair that had shimmered around her face only seconds before was now plastered to the side of her head.

"Perhaps you can make an appointment and come back sometime next week," Miss T. said kindly, but the children could hear laughter lurking just beneath her words.

"Perhaps," Tawny managed to sputter. She stomped angrily out to the van, followed by the two men. The van door slammed open and Tawny took off her coat and threw it inside, all the while digging snow out from under her collar. "Get this thing started," she spit out, "before I freeze to death!"

The van's engine roared to life and its tires spun on the slick snow before they finally caught and the van jerked down the drive and headed back toward town.

"Merry Christmas!" Nick shouted.

Addie collapsed with laughter in the snow and Brian leaned against the house, holding his sides.

Miss T. stood at the back door and her face was puckered in an attempt not to smile at the giggling children. Nick's dark eyes sparkled and he gave her an ornery grin. "Sorry about that," he said.

"I'll bet you are," Miss T. said dryly.

The sound of another car coming down the drive silenced them all. It was the Bradys' car this time and Nick was puzzled.

"What's my dad doing here?"

The car stopped and Mr. Brady and his companion stepped out. Addie didn't recognize the other man.

But with a gasp and a whoop, Brian flew past Addie and threw himself into the arms of his father.

CHAPTER 2

Unexpected Plans

Mr. Dennison hugged his son tightly for several moments and it gave Addie a good opportunity to observe the two together. She was surprised at what she saw. Brian didn't resemble his father at all. Brian had dark blond hair and brown eyes, but Brad Dennison had coppery red hair and green eyes. He was a handsome man with a warm smile.

Brian must look like his mom, Addie concluded to herself. Mrs. Dennison had died two years ago.

"How ya doing, Nick?" Mr. Dennison asked. He pulled Nick close and gave the boy a hug.

"Great!" Nick grinned. "Just great."

Then the older man looked over to Addie and smiled broadly. "Hi, Addie," he said. "What a pleasure to finally meet you! Brian writes about you and Nick all the time."

"Hi, Mr. Dennison," she answered shyly. "He talks about you a lot, too."

"I can't believe you're here," Brian said, and his smile still split his face. "I thought you were going to send for me after Christmas. Sometime in January."

Mr. Dennison shrugged. "I couldn't wait. I missed you too much," he said simply.

Brian blinked hard and swallowed. "I missed you, too," he murmured.

"Well," Mr. Brady said a bit too loudly. "I hate to break up your afternoon of fun, kids, but I think Brian would like to spend some time with his dad, wouldn't you, Brian?"

Brian nodded and Nick said, "I can't wait to hear all about Japan!"

"And you will," Mr. Brady agreed, "but not today. Brad is going to drop you and me off at home, and he and Brian are going in town for dinner."

Nick's smile drooped but he nodded. "That's a good idea. I bet you've got a lot to talk about."

"You want a ride home, Addie?"

Miss T. spoke up. "I'm baking cookies, miss, if you want to stay and help," she offered.

Addie grinned. "Chocolate chip?"

"What else?" the elderly woman laughed.

The two men and their sons left, and Addie spent the rest of the afternoon eating cookie dough with Miss T. and Amy, Miss T.'s hired companion. The time sped by and soon Mr. McCormick was in the driveway and Addie was on her way home with a plateful of warm, moist cookies.

"Mmm, boy, are these good," her father said between bites.

"Brian's dad is back from Japan!" Addie announced as they got on their way.

"I know," her father mumbled and a chunk of cookie fell off in his lap.

"When did you find out?" Addie demanded. "Did you know he was coming when you took us to Miss T.'s?"

"Yep."

"Dad!"

"They wanted Brian to be totally surprised, so we decided to go on with our plans as if nothing out of the ordinary was going to happen."

"He was surprised, all right," Addie said. "It's going to be a nice Christmas for him."

"It'll be different, that's for sure," her father replied.

"What do you mean?"

Mr. McCormick looked quickly at his daughter. "Didn't they tell you?"

"Tell me what?"

"Brian and his dad are leaving day after tomorrow. They'll visit some relatives in Ohio for a few days, and then be in Japan on Christmas Eve."

Addie stared straight ahead. "I thought... they'd leave ... in January," she said faintly. "Or at least after Christmas."

Mr. McCormick shook his head and took Addie's hand. "I'm sorry, sweetheart. I thought they'd told you. Mr. Dennison has to get back before Christmas. He's very close to signing a deal with some big-wigs over there and the deal has to be closed before the end of the year."

Addie just shrugged and looked out her window. "It's okay, Dad," she said, but it wasn't okay.

Although she'd moved several times herself, she'd never had a friend move away from her. It was a strange feeling and she didn't think she liked it.

* * *

Nick didn't like it either. The next morning he and Addie were building a snowman in Nick's front yard. Brian and his father had gone into town again, this time to buy Brian some new clothes before they left. Jesse Kate, Nick's baby sister, was outside with them.

"I can't believe they're doing this," Nick grumbled. "I mean, they didn't even give us any warning!"

"We knew he'd be leaving in January," Addie reminded him.

"Yeah, but that's *January*," Nick said. "That's way far away."

"Two whole weeks."

Nick tossed a handful of snow at his friend. "You know what I mean. Even if it is only two weeks, I was prepared for it." He paused. "I'm not prepared for this."

"Me neither," Addie agreed.

"It would help if Brian was even a little bit sad about it," Nick complained. "But he's so happy, it's disgusting."

Addie giggled. "Come on, Nick, don't be selfish. He missed his dad."

"I don't think he's going to miss me a bit."

"Sure, he will," Addie reassured her friend. "But you can't blame him for wanting to be with his father. Be honest. Wouldn't you miss your family if you had to live away from them?"

"I'm not sure," Nick mumbled as he tromped across the yard to pull Jesse Kate out of a snow drift she had buried her face in. "Come on, Jess, don't do that. You'll freeze your nose off."

The active toddler had discovered the joy of eating snow. But she was so bundled up she couldn't put her arms down at her sides, and her oversized mittens kept her from picking anything up with her hands. So she resorted to plopping down on her well-padded bottom and then falling over onto her face to get at the powdery snack.

"You'd miss her a lot," Addie laughed.

"Yeah, right." Nick carried the little girl over to the half-built snowman while she smacked his cheeks playfully with her wet mittens. "Stay here and help me and Addie," he commanded.

She smiled agreeably, so he sat her down. She waddled away faster than he could stop her, dropped to her knees, and fell on her face once more.

"Jess!" Nick shouted in frustration.

"It's okay, Nick," Mrs. Brady called from the back door. She came down the steps without a coat and stopped at the edge of the sidewalk. "Come here, honey," she called to the little girl. "Time to come inside, now. Mommy needs your help." She clapped her hands and held out her arms.

"She won't come," Nick grumbled. "She never does what you want."

As if to prove her big brother wrong, Jesse waddled quickly to her mother's outstretched arms and waved goodbye as they headed for the house.

"Oh, I almost forgot why I came to get Jesse," Mrs. Brady said and came back to the edge of the yard. "Miss T. just called. She wants you children to come see her this afternoon. She has something she wants to ask you. Your mom is coming to take you out there, Addie."

"But Brian's not here," Nick protested.

Mrs. Brady smiled. "I don't think this involves Brian, hon," she said.

"What's going on?" he asked Addie.

She shrugged. "I don't know, but I guess we'll find out soon enough. There's my mom now."

Mrs. McCormick honked and waved at Mrs. Brady while Nick and Addie brushed themselves off and climbed in the car.

"What's up, Mom?" Addie asked.

Mrs. McCormick only smiled. "I think you'd better wait and talk to Eunice."

"So you know what's going on, you just won't tell us," Nick surmised, but Mrs. McCormick laughed and refused to say anything else.

When they got to Miss T.'s house, the elderly woman was watching for them from her kitchen window. Addie's mom stopped the car and followed the children inside.

"Come in, come in," Miss T. said. She motioned to the chairs around her table and they all sat down. Nick helped himself to a cookie from the cookie jar.

"Well, miss, I can tell from your face I'd better get right to the point," Miss T. laughed. "Your parents tell me Brian is leaving for Japan tomorrow."

Addie frowned and nodded.

"And I'm sure you're going to miss him a great deal."

They both nodded this time.

"Would you like to do something to take your mind off your woes?" she asked.

"Like what?" Nick asked cautiously.

"Well, I'm sure you're aware that the Kensington Museum for the Performing Arts in Chicago is opening its exhibit of Tierny Bryce momentos this weekend." Miss T.'s identity had been discovered partly because she had sold many of the momentos she'd saved from her days in Hollywood. The entire collection was touring museums around the country. "They've asked me to speak at the opening on Sunday night."

"You mean you're leaving too?" Nick complained.

"Only for a few days," Miss T. smiled. "And Amy and I could use some company."

Addie's eyes grew wide as she looked from Miss T. to her mother and back to Miss T. "Us?" she asked incredulously.

Her mother nodded.

"You mean—*just* us?"

Her mother laughed and nodded again.

Nick was skeptical. "Do my folks know about this?" he asked.

"They sure do," Miss T. said.

"And they agreed?" he managed to squeak out.

"They sure did."

Addie and Nick stared at one another in disbelief. Then Addie burst out excitedly, "Yes, *Yes*, YES!"

"Chicago," Nick breathed. "Alone!"

CHAPTER 3

Goodbye, Brian—
Hello, Chicago

"Not quite alone," Addie's mom said.

Nick gave Mrs. McCormick an apologetic smile. "Oh, I know," he said hastily. "I just meant without...parents."

"But not without supervision," Miss T. said firmly. "Of course, Amy and I will be there. But we thought it might be a good idea to have another young person to keep track of you two. So Amy's nephew Sam will meet us at our hotel and help us find our way around the city. He's a freshman at the University of Chicago."

"Great!" Nick exclaimed. Then his expression saddened. "I just wish Brian could go along."

"Brian is going to be very happy where he's going, and a trip to Chicago should take your minds off his absence," Mrs. McCormick said kindly. "So let's be grateful the Lord has blessed everyone so abundantly this Christmas, okay?"

Addie and Nick nodded, and Addie gave Miss T. a big hug. "Thanks a lot, Miss T. I think this is going to be a wonderful vacation!"

"Me, too," Nick agreed and gave the elderly woman a quick squeeze. "When do we leave?"

"Thursday morning, bright and early. Willard is driving us to Chicago at eight o'clock. He's got business that afternoon, so I thought it would be easier to ride with him than to take one of the charter flights from Rankin's Air Field."

"And Dad and I will drive up Monday morning to pick you up," Mrs. McCormick added. "So you'll be home on Christmas Eve."

Addie stood up suddenly. "We've got to get home and pack if we're leaving day after tomorrow!"

"What's to pack?" Nick frowned. "Throw a couple of pair of jeans into a suitcase, some sweatshirts, socks, underwear, toothbrush—what else is there?"

Addie rolled her eyes, and Miss T. put a gentle arm around Nick's shoulders. "You'll have to have a suit and tie, sir. The opening is a formal event. And jeans and sweatshirts are fine for sightseeing, but nice pants and sweaters are a must when we eat out in the evenings."

Nick stared woefully at his elderly friend. "We're dressing up *every night?*"

Miss T. nodded.

Nick's expression brightened. "I don't think I've got that many good clothes," he said.

"I've already talked with your mother and she's started packing for you," Miss T. informed him.

"Oh." Nick took a deep breath and straightened up. "I guess I can stand it for a few days," he said with a sigh.

Addie played a pretend violin. "What a noble sacrifice," she teased her friend.

Nick made a face and pointed a finger at her. *"You've* never worn a tie," he said.

"And *you've* never worn pantyhose," she countered.

Nick grinned. "Good point," he said.

Addie and Nick talked nonstop in the car on the way back from Miss T.'s. Addie's mom dropped Nick off at his house and then drove the last mile home.

"I've never been away from you and Dad for more than one night before," Addie said softly.

Her mother nodded. "We're going to miss you."

Addie sighed. "Especially before Christmas. Who's going to do the Christmas cards?" For as long as she could remember, it had been Addie's job to open and read the Christmas cards they received each day, then hang them around the door frames all through the house.

"Would you like me to save the rest of them until you get back?"

Addie smiled gratefully at her mother. "Would you? Then we could open them together on Christmas Eve."

"Of course, honey." Mrs. McCormick squeezed her daughter's hand. "You know, your dad and I would never have agreed to this if we didn't think you were old enough to handle it. We trust you."

"Thanks, Mom."

* * *

Brian and his father left the next morning. Mr. Dennison had rented a car to drive to Ohio to visit his family. Addie and her father sped down to the Bradys' house shortly after seven to see them off.

The early morning air was so cold it almost hurt to take a deep breath, so goodbyes were quick—but still hard. Nick and Brian exchanged a brief hug, with promises to write. Addie gave Brian a short, embarrased hug and he grinned shyly at her.

"Keep Nick in line, will you?" he said. "No food fights in those fancy restaurants in Chicago!"

They all laughed at the memory of a cafeteria food fight Nick had instigated early in the school year. Nick gave Brian a friendly shove while the adults shook hands. Then the Dennisons were gone, tooting their horn softly as they sped away down the country road.

There was little opportunity to be sad, though. Last minute packing took all of Addie's time and even most of Nick's. There wasn't an extra tube of toothpaste to be had in the McCormick household and even though Nick searched for the better part of an hour, he couldn't find the match to his warmest pair of mittens. A quick trip to town for the needed items capped off the day. When Addie finally dropped into bed that night, she fell asleep quickly and dreamed of busy streets and tall buildings and an elegant restaurant that served only chocolate chip cookies.

* * *

Addie was up at dawn the next morning and dressed and ready to go by seven o'clock. Her mother was already in the kitchen, cooking a big breakfast, and her father joined them five minutes later.

"Must be a big day if you're out of bed before ten o'clock," Mr. McCormick teased his daughter. "Nervous?"

Addie nodded. "Just a little bit," she admitted. "I woke up early and started thinking about a lot of things and then I couldn't get back to sleep."

"What kind of things?" her mother asked.

"Well, for starters, I've never met Willard. I don't think Miss T. likes him very much. Why is he driving us to Chicago?"

Her father laughed. "Oh, Miss T. likes him. He's the only one in Francine's family she can't intimidate, though, so she grumbles about him. I've talked with him several times. He's a nice guy. You'll like him. What else?"

"Where will I sleep?" Addie asked. "With Miss T. and Amy? And what about Nick? He will *not* want to share a room with three females. And how will we get around Chicago? Will we have to take cabs everywhere? And what about money? Will I need any money?"

The myriad of questions Addie had been pondering since five o'clock that morning poured out in a nervous stream, and her father reached out and pulled her down on his lap.

"It's okay, kiddo," he said softly and kissed the top of her head. "I didn't realize there were so many things worrying you. Let me see if I can't answer some of them.

"I imagine you and Miss T. and Amy will share a room. Nick will probably be right next door with Amy's nephew. And I believe the museum hired a limousine for you while you're in Chicago, so you won't have to worry about cabs.

"As for money, Miss T. has insisted on paying all your expenses, but your mom and I are sending some extra cash with you anyway. I'm sure you'll want to buy a couple of souvenirs, and probably some pop or a candy bar. And I think it would be a good idea if you and Nick went together and bought Miss T. and Amy each a small thank you gift."

He paused. "So. Anything else?"

Addie shook her head and hugged her dad hard. "Thanks, Dad. I'm going to miss you."

Her father laughed. "The time is going to go so fast, you'll barely remember you've got parents until we're there to pick you up Monday morning. Now, let's eat some of that sausage and French toast."

An hour later, Willard's blue Chevy pulled into the McCormicks' drive and Nick hopped out of the back seat. He ran to the door and Addie met him, suitcase in hand.

"Ready?" he grinned. Addie nodded and turned back to her parents.

"Why don't we pray before you head out?" Mr. McCormick said. Without waiting for an answer, he put one hand on Nick's shoulder and an arm around Addie. "Lord, thank You for this opportunity for Nick and Addie to have a special Christmas vacation. I ask for Your protection and deliverance for everyone as they drive to Chicago. Please watch over them as they sightsee in the Windy City and bless the time they spend with Eunice and Amy. Thank You again, Lord, for all the special things You do for us. We pray all this in Jesus' name. Amen."

"Amens" echoed softly in the room and Addie hugged her parents one more time. "Don't forget to save the Christmas cards," she reminded her mother and stopped short. "I forgot to get the mail yesterday!" she exclaimed.

"I got it," her mother smiled, "and I've already set the cards in that basket." She pointed to a brightly decorated Christmas basket on the counter.

Addie glanced at the new stack of envelopes and gave a frustrated sigh. "Katie and Taku's Christmas letter, and I have to wait until next week to read it." Katie and Taku were missionaries Addie's parents had supported for many years. Their letters were always interesting and Addie loved reading about their life in Nagaland, a small territory in India.

"Take it with you, then," her mother said and handed her the card. "Read it before you go to bed tonight."

"Thanks, Mom," she said and tucked the long white envelope in her coat pocket.

They all walked out to the car, and Addie and Nick crawled in the back seat next to Amy. Addie's mother blew her one last kiss and the car pulled out of the drive. The McCormicks stood outside and waved and Addie watched them until the car turned the corner and her parents disappeared from sight.

The ride to Chicago was a fun one, largely because of Willard. He was a small man with a fat stomach and thinning grey hair. His smile was big and his laugh was bigger, and he kept them all entertained with stories about his travels as a salesman for The Exotic Pet company.

They made two bathroom stops and one drive-through for a Coke and some fries and the two-and-a-half hour trip to Chicago passed quickly. Soon they were off Interstate 57 and on the expressway. Nick was the first to recognize a famous landmark.

"Look!" he exclaimed with his nose pressed to the window. "It's the new Comiskey Park!"

"What's that?" Miss T. asked.

Nick stared at her in disbelief. "Comiskey Park? It's where the White Sox play."

"Oh." Miss T. nodded wisely and glanced at Addie. *Baseball?* she mouthed to the young girl. Addie grinned and nodded.

A heavy, bluish smog hung over the city, fading in and out among the panorama of skyscrapers that appeared in the distance. Traffic had increased steadily since they'd exited the interstate. Cars were zipping by them on their left, and drivers weaved in and out of lanes at an alarming speed.

"How much longer until we get to the hotel?" Miss T. asked nervously.

Willard shrugged. "Depends on the traffic downtown."

The elderly woman leaned against her headrest and closed her eyes. "Wake me when we get there," she said.

Willard only laughed. "Don't think about the traffic. Just pretend you're in a giant parking lot that's moving down the road at about 70 miles an hour!"

"Is that how fast we're going?" Nick asked.

Willard didn't answer, but the car slowed down just a little and Addie noticed more people passing them on the left.

They drove down Eisenhower and under an immense building with about a million windows that spanned all the lanes of traffic. "What's that?" Addie asked.

"Post office," Willard answered and Addie started to laugh.

"What's so funny?" Nick asked.

"I was just thinking about our post office," Addie said.

Nick grinned. "Yeah. My dad can stand in front of the postmaster's window and touch all four walls!"

Minutes later, they were in downtown Chicago and Addie gasped. "Nick, look!" She pointed to the corner of Kinzie and Kingsbury, and Nick gaped at a five-story mural of Michael Jordan dressed in an elegant suit.

"Cool," he breathed.

"Well, this has gone better than I thought," Willard said. "We're about a block from your hotel and this is the first time traffic's been backed up. Must be something going on. Look at all the people."

Addie and Nick both leaned forward to stare out the front window. People lined the street. Although all the sidewalks had been crowded since they'd gotten into Chicago, here the people seemed to be standing still.

"What are they waiting for?" Nick asked.

"Beats me," Willard said. "Whatever it is, you'll get to see it. They're lined up right to the front door of your hotel." He pointed down the street to a elegant white building with huge glass doors.

Willard peered over the steering wheel. "Would you look at—" He sat up sharply. "Lock your doors—now!"

At his sudden change of voice, no one hesitated, and four hands slammed down four locks almost simultaneously. They weren't a moment too soon, either. Addie suddenly heard a woman's voice scream, "There she is!" and their car was quickly surrounded by smiling, waving people, pounding on their doors and windows.

A middle-aged woman pressed her face against Miss T.'s window. "Miss Bryce, please sign this for me!" In her hand she held an early publicity photo of Winston Rinehart and Tierny Bryce. Policemen tried unsuccessfully to keep the crowd back, and their car came to a complete standstill.

Willard whistled softly. "Welcome to Chicago, Tierny Bryce."

CHAPTER 4

Jean-Luc's

"This is crazy!" Nick exclaimed. He waved at a young boy with coal black hair and big brown eyes who was standing outside his door, grinning and waving another photo. Nick began to roll down his window.

"Leave it up," Willard said firmly. "I know these people have good intentions, but I don't want an over-zealous fan pulling one of you out the window."

Miss T. turned to Willard. "Get us out of here!" she said impatiently.

Willard laughed. "Just where do you want me to go? And which group of people should I run over?"

Miss T. sighed and waved politely at an older man holding a placard which had the words, "We love you, Tierny Bryce!" printed in bold black letters.

"Who's that?" Addie pointed to a very distinguished man in an expensive suit pushing his way through the crowd to Willard's side of the car.

Willard rolled his window down a crack and the man smiled warmly and shouted, "Welcome to

Jean-Luc's! My name is Victor Francis. I'm the hotel manager. We were expecting a crowd, but this is a bit overwhelming, isn't it?"

Miss T. spoke sharply, "A bit."

"The valet by the entrance is waiting to help Miss Bryce out of the car and into the hotel," he told Willard. "There's another valet at the corner of the building who will show you where to park. Just proceed slowly and the people will move. I'll be waiting inside to show you to your suite."

Victor gestured to the police who were still keeping an eye on the crowd. They made a concerted effort to move people away from the car and off the street and Willard was able to pull into the circular drive in front of the hotel. There the sidewalks had been cordoned off so the crowd couldn't reach the car. The valet opened Miss T.'s door and helped the elderly woman out. A deafening roar greeted Tierny Bryce.

"Wait!" she called to Willard, but her voice was lost in the din.

"We'll meet you inside," he called back. The valet slammed the door and Willard pulled slowly around the drive and back onto the street.

Addie and Nick watched through the back window as they pulled away. There were half-a-dozen news teams waiting near the door, and people were almost falling over the ropes around the sidewalk in their effort to reach Miss T.

Now that Tierny Bryce was out of the car, no one paid any attention to them. Willard followed another valet down a service drive next to the hotel and parked near a back entrance. A tall blond woman greeted them there.

"Hello, Mr. Sadler," she said and shook hands with Willard. "Welcome to Jean-Luc's. My name is Marcia Vetter. And you must be Amy." She extended her hand and Amy shook it. "Welcome."

Amy smiled. "Thank you, Marcia. Has my nephew, Sam, arrived?"

Marcia shook her head. "No, but he's called. He'll be here after lunch. And that leaves Addie and Nick. Hi, kids. How are you?"

Nick gave Marcia a suspicious frown. "How do you know our names?"

She grinned and winked. "It's my job," she said. "Come on," she continued in a conspiratorial whisper. "We're sneaking you upstairs to your suite."

"Why do we have to sneak?" Addie asked.

"Yeah, no one knows who we are," Nick added.

"I'm afraid that will change once people get a good look at your faces," Marcia told them. "You two are something of a curiosity to Miss Bryce's fans. They're eager to meet the kids who gave them back their idol." Nick and Addie exchanged guilty grins. "But don't worry about that," Marcia continued. "*You're* here to have fun, and *I'm* here to see that you do. So, we sneak."

She opened a heavy steel door into the hotel and led them down a long corridor with grey and white linoleum. Doors lined both sides of the corridor and the children peered into each one. The first opened into a huge laundry, the next to the kitchen, and the next to a room filled with pipes and compressors and loud noises.

"This is the service center of the hotel," Marcia explained. "We're taking the service elevator to your floor. No one will see us except the employees."

They went around a corner and came face to face with the little boy with black hair and brown eyes that Nick had tried to talk with earlier.

Marcia sighed. "Rico, I told you not to come by today. We're very busy."

"Aw, Marcia, cut me some slack," the youngster begged. "Ain't every day ya got kids here." He took off the Bulls cap he was wearing and turned it around.

"Hi, Rico," Nick said.

"Hey, dude," Rico said. He held out his hand, palm up, and Nick slapped it.

"Who let you in this time?" Marcia asked.

Rico grinned. "She looked familiar, but . . . her name escapes me."

"Yeah, yeah," Marcia said with a sigh. "Really, Rico, you've got to go. Maybe we can see you later tonight or tomorrow.

Rico shrugged. "Sure, Marcia. Anything you say." He gave Addie and Nick another grin. "Later."

He disappeared around the corner and Marcia gestured toward an elevator door that had just slid open with a soft "ping pong." They all stepped inside.

"Your assistants will bring your luggage to the suite," Marcia told them.

"Our assistants?" Nick asked.

"Yes. Each of you has been assigned a personal assistant—one of our employees who will work only with you. I'll introduce you to them later."

"Who's Rico?" Addie inquired.

Marcia smiled a sad smile. "Rico is—Rico," she said. "None of us know his last name. He's a kid who showed up about a year ago. The staff took a liking to him and someone always lets him inside. I'm afraid he sweet talks a lot of our patrons out of their spare change. But most of our regulars ask about him whenever they're in town, so we don't discourage him too much."

"Maybe he can show us around," Nick suggested.

Marcia's eyes widened. "I'm not sure you'd want to see what Rico can show you. His family is very poor and he helps his mother raise four more brothers, all younger than he is. Hustling the wealthy people who come to our hotel is only one of his jobs, I'm afraid. He's very . . . street smart."

The elevator "ponged" open into a large, bright, antiseptic-looking room. Everything was white and chrome and the floor sparkled. There were maids loading long carts with sheets and towels. Under the carts were sliding doors with chrome handles and when a maid opened one of them, Addie saw buckets and sponges and cleaning supplies of all kinds. The whole place smelled like the pine cleaner Addie's mom used to clean the bathroom. Marcia opened another large steel door and they stepped out of that room and into another world.

The hall was spacious with smoky blue carpet that was so plush you sank into it with every step. There were no lights overhead, only brass lamps on the walls that cast a soft pinkish light. Every few yards there was a small table set against the wall and each table held a large vase of fresh-cut flowers. Addie stopped to smell every bouquet.

Nick pulled her impatiently from the fourth one and whispered in her ear. "Where are the rooms? There aren't any doors."

Marcia heard his whisper and smiled. "This is the penthouse floor, Nick. We only have two suites here, one on this side of the building and one on the other. So there's only one door and it's right here." She stopped in front of a large door with no door-knob.

"We have the whole floor to ourselves?" Addie asked.

Marcia nodded. "This side, anyway. We have another guest on the other side." She pulled a small gold card from her pocket and slipped it into a slot at the edge of the door. The door opened silently and slid into the wall. "Here's your suite."

Addie, Amy, Willard, and Nick filed into the room, and Addie could feel her heart begin to pound. It was a large sitting room, bigger than her living room at home, and it was decorated in soft, rosy pinks and smoky blues. There were over-stuffed, high backed chairs and the longest sofa, filled with fluffy pillows, that Addie had ever seen.

A long, low coffee table sat in front of the sofa. It held a variety of magazines and another large bouquet of fresh flowers. A deep walnut cabinet filled one wall of the room.

"This is the entertainment center," Marcia explained. "It has a CD player, a large screen television, and a VCR." She opened the cabinet door to reveal a four-foot by four-foot screen and Nick whistled.

"You also have televisions in your rooms," she said with a smile. She opened a door to the left of the entertainment center. "Nick, here's where you and Sam will sleep," she said. Nick peered into the room and his mouth dropped open.

"And here's your room, Addie," she said, and opened a door to the right.

Addie stepped through the door. A king-sized, four-poster waterbed with a canopy, curtains, and big pillows sat in the middle of the room. An oak table, with more flowers and four chairs, sat inside a large bay window that opened onto an enclosed balcony. Another television was encased in a cabinet on the wall, and there was a huge bathroom with a walk-in closet that had rows of drawers and what seemed to be a hundred hangers. On the fourth wall was a huge painting of a lake full of white lilies. Addie stood next to the bed in a daze.

Nick came running into the room. "Cool! You've got a balcony." Addie nodded.

"I've got an exercise room!" Nick exclaimed.

"What?" Addie finally found her voice.

"Come see," Nick urged her.

She followed him into the sitting room and tossed her purse on the sofa before entering his room. It was even larger than hers, but it had to be, because this room held *two* king-sized waterbeds, a table and chairs, and opened into a small exercise room with a weight bench, a step-climber, and an exercise bike.

"This is incredible," she said faintly.

"I'll say," Nick agreed. "I wonder what Miss T.'s room looks like."

"Let's go see," Addie said. They ran out of Nick's room and into the sitting room. A delicate chime sounded so Addie crossed the room to the hall door. There was no knob on the inside either, but a small panel to the left held several buttons, one of which said "Open." Addie pushed it and the door slid open.

A maid with a cart stood outside. The cart held steaming cups of hot chocolate with a small bowl of marshmallows on the side. Marcia and Amy came out of the bedroom and Marcia frowned. "We haven't ordered food yet," she said.

"Mr. Francis sent a warm beverage for the children," the maid answered.

"Fine," Marcia said. "Just leave it, Carmen. Thank you."

"Can we see your room, Amy?" Nick asked.

"Of course," Amy said. She led the children into the master bedroom. It was the size of Addie's and Nick's rooms combined. There was a huge fireplace on one wall and a gas fire crackled merrily. There was another balcony, similar to Addie's, two more canopied waterbeds, a bath with a jacuzzi and a walk-in closet, a dining area, and a small sitting area with more chairs and a small sofa. Overhead, a skylight flooded the room with sun.

"This is the life!" Nick proclaimed, and Amy and Willard laughed. Then they heard the soft, almost imperceptible sound of the door sliding open in the next room.

"Miss T.!" Addie exclaimed and she and Nick ran to the sitting room. But there was no one there, although the door clicked shut just as they arrived. "Who was that?" she questioned Marcia, who had joined them.

Marcia looked puzzled, but she smiled. "It must have been a maid. Only they have access to these rooms." She pushed the open button on the panel and they all peered out into the hallway. No one was in sight and Marcia frowned. "That's strange. Our employees are fast, but not that fast," she joked. "I hope these doors aren't malfunctioning."

Addie stepped out into the hall and looked up and down the corridor. At the far end of the hall, she saw the flash of a dirty white high-topped sneaker disappear around the corner.

CHAPTER 5

Who's Who?

Marcia stepped into the corridor behind Addie. "Did you see anyone?" she asked.

Addie hesitated. "I—I don't know," she finally said. "I thought I saw someone go around the corner." She pointed down the hall.

Marcia frowned. "Must have been a maid. Oh, well. Why don't we go back in and wait for—"

At that moment, Addie heard an elevator chime around the opposite corner and Miss T.'s familiar voice carried all the way down the hall.

"—absolutely cannot continue. Those people almost knocked me over! I'm too old for this—"

"No, you're not," Addie called out, and Miss T. came around the corner with a frown on her face and fire in her eyes.

"Don't tell me I'm not old," she snapped at the young girl, but reached out and gave her a quick hug anyway. "I'm glad to see you're all right. Where's Nick?"

"Right here," Nick called from the suite. "Say, can I have your auto—"

"Don't start with me, young man," Miss T. entered the room and wagged a finger in his face, "or I'll autograph your bottom! You're not too old—" She stopped short and looked around at her opulent surroundings. "Oh, my."

"Pretty cool, huh?" Nick flopped onto the sofa and pulled the cart with the hot chocolate next to him.

"Be careful with that," Miss T. said absent-mindedly, turning in circles to look at the whole room.

"And watch out for my purse," Addie said.

"What purse?" Nick looked around him on the sofa. "Here it is." He picked Addie's small leather bag up off the floor and handed it to her.

The bag was open and Addie's heart skipped a beat as she searched frantically for the billfold that held the 50 dollars her father had given her before they left home. It was there, tucked safely in the zippered side pocket where she'd put it that morning.

"Now, where's my change purse?" she murmured to herself. She pulled the rest of the purse's contents out, but the change purse was gone. "Nick, is my change purse on the—Nick?" Addie looked up to find herself alone in the room. Everyone else was giving Miss T. a tour of their suite.

So Addie checked on the sofa and under the cushions and on the floor and around the coffee table. But her change purse was nowhere in sight and Addie dropped into one of the high-backed chairs with a sigh.

"I guess it wasn't that much money," she said to no one in particular.

"What?" Nick asked as they all came out of his bedroom "Talking to yourself, Addie?"

"I lost my change purse," she told him.

"With all your money?" Miss T was concerned.

Addie shook her head. "Just a couple of dollars in change, that's all."

"Maybe it's in the car," Willard suggested. "I'll check when I leave and if it's there, I'll give it to your personal assistant," he teased.

"Her what?" Miss T. asked.

"Her personal assistant," Nick said in a lofty tone. "We all get one. In case we need...assistance."

Miss T. shook her head. "No personal assistants. We can take care of ourselves," she said firmly.

"You might find it's easier to have one of our employees run some of your errands," Marcia suggested tactfully. "Do you really want to face that crowd everytime you need something?"

Miss T. frowned. "We'll find some way around that, I can guarantee you. I'm not staying cooped up in this suite—not matter how nice it is—for an entire weekend. And I'm not getting mobbed everytime I go out, either. We'll think of something. Don't think we won't."

Marcia hesitated, then smiled. "All right," she said. "I'll cancel the assistants. But please, let *me* know if there's any way I can help you. And one of our limousines has been reserved for your personal use all weekend."

"That should be inconspicuous," Nick murmured and Addie giggled.

Marcia grinned at the two children. "Dial 221 if you need me," was all she said. She pushed the button to open the door and a second or two later, it slid shut silently behind her.

"How does it do that?" Nick wanted to know.

"I think it's electronic," Willard answered. "To open the door you have to use a card or push the button, but it will close automatically after it senses the last person is through."

"How does it know when that is?"

"It has an electronic eye that senses anything solid. When nothing solid is passing through the door, it waits a second or so and then closes."

"So there's no chance of getting squished," Nick concluded.

Willard grinned. "Probably not."

"Good. I'm hungry." Nick changed the subject abruptly and Addie laughed, but her growling stomach quickly concurred and Miss T. ordered room service for the five of them. Within minutes, a cart filled with plates of food arrived at their door. The two maids who brought the cart set the table in Miss T.'s suite. Everyone sat down and Amy said a quick blessing.

There were hamburgers so fat and juicy Addie could hardly get her mouth around them. They were delicious, but Addie was a little disappointed.

"I thought Jean-Luc's was a French hotel," she said. "Will we get to eat any French food?"

Nick tossed a fry onto her plate. "There you go," he said. "Eat up." Addie made a face at him and Amy laughed.

"We can try whatever you want," Miss T. assured her young friend. "Although a good hamburger always hits the spot for me. And look what we have for dessert!"

She lifted the lid off a fancy silver platter. It was filled with chocolate chip cookies and a note from Marcia that said, "Enjoy, Addie!"

"I don't believe it!" Nick burst out. "How does she *know* these things?"

"Who cares?" Addie said and took the cookie on top.

Amy excused herself and went to the phone in the sitting room. While she was there, Addie, Nick, and Miss T. discussed what they would do that afternoon.

"Have you ever been to Shedd's Aquarium?" Addie said. "It's fantastic! They have a huge circular tank and you can watch all kinds of fish and sharks and turtles. They even have a diver who goes in every day to feed the fish. He's got a microphone in his mask and he talks to you while he's feeding them."

"That sounds cool," Nick agreed. "Let's go there."

Addie hesitated. "But what about you, Miss T.? Do you think people will recognize you?"

Amy came back into the room and sat down with a smile. "I might have a solution to that problem," she said. "That is, if you're game, Eunice."

"I'll try anything once," Miss T. said. "What do I have to do?"

"Hang on," Nick interrupted. "Can I wear jeans to this aquarium? I'm going to die if I have to wear good pants and shoes all day." Nick's mother had made him dress in nice clothes for the trip to Chicago.

"Of course you can," Miss T. said. "Why don't you change while Amy and I talk?"

Nick and Addie both left the room, Nick to change his clothes and Addie to brush her teeth. Just as she finished brushing, she heard the door chime, so she rinsed her mouth quickly and ran to answer it.

Marcia stood in the doorway, holding a brown paper grocery sack. She grinned broadly at Addie.

"This is going to be fun!" she exclaimed.

"What?" Addie asked.

"Didn't they tell you?" Marcia asked. Addie shook her head. "Then I'll wait and we'll surprise you." She knocked on Miss T.'s door and went inside.

"What's going on?" Nick emerged from his room in jeans and a sweatshirt and nodded toward the door.

Addie shrugged. "I guess we'll find out when they're finished," she said.

They didn't have to wait long. Soon Miss T. came out of her room. Her face was covered by the brim of a big black hat Addie had seen her wear to church and she was wrapping her black leather coat around her.

"What are we doing, Miss T.?" Addie asked and the woman raised her head.

But it was Marcia's face that grinned out from beneath the hat. "I guess it works, huh?" she said.

Even as Addie and Nick gaped at the woman disguised as Miss T., Miss T. came out the door herself and this time Nick shouted with laughter.

The elegant Tierny Bryce was decked out in a fuzzy brown wool coat that made her look much heavier than she really was. The straight grey hair that was always pulled back in a bun was covered with a short, curly salt-and-pepper wig. She had a tattered brown scarf over her head and around her neck, and big wire rim glasses magnified her blue eyes and made her look like an owl. She smiled triumphantly at the two laughing children. Amy stood behind her, chuckling.

"Sam is waiting downstairs in his Volkswagen to take us to the aquarium," Amy informed the children. "Marcia is going to take a ride around the block in the limousine to confuse anyone who might see us leaving."

"You're still going out the service entrance," Marcia said. "But I wouldn't be surprised if your fans have staked out the back door already. If there is someone there, they should be distracted by the commotion I cause at the front door."

Addie and Nick ran to get their coats and they left the suite. Marcia went down the public elevator with Victor Francis, the hotel manager. The children, Amy, and Willard showed Miss T. the door to the service room and they rode that elevator to the ground floor.

Willard gave his elderly aunt a quick peck on the cheek. "You look classy, Eunice," he teased. "Have fun this weekend." He waved goodbye to the children and trotted down the drive to his car.

Sam Tanaka sat next to the back door of the hotel in a shiny metallic blue Volkswagen Golf. Sam was handsome, with straight black hair and sparkling black eyes. He reached over and opened the front door for Miss T. She climbed in quickly and Addie, Nick, and Amy squeezed into the small back seat.

Willard pulled down the drive ahead of them and tooted his horn softly. They all waved and he stopped to look both ways before pulling out into the busy street. Even from where they sat, they could hear the cry that went up from the crowd in front of the door of the hotel.

"That's the car she came in!" someone shouted and a wave of people surged down the sidewalk toward Willard's Chevy. His tires squealed as he pulled out in front of them and sped down the busy street. About 50 people followed him, but another 50 or so saw the long white limousine pulling into the circular drive. They ran back to see "Tierny Bryce" duck into the back seat and speed down the street after Willard.

With their idol gone, the crowd dispersed quickly and the sidewalk was clear when the little blue Volkswagen pulled out and turned the opposite direction.

Once they were underway, Sam extended his hand to Miss T. "Hi. My name's Clyde. You're Bonnie, I presume?"

They all laughed and Miss T. shook his hand as they sped away from fame and fortune and headed for Lake Shore Drive.

CHAPTER 6

The Sights of Chicago

"Now for the real test," said Miss T. They were standing in a large parking lot behind the Field Museum, ready to head for Shedd's Aquarium. "How do I look?"

"Like my third grade teacher, Miss Waldmeyer," Nick grinned.

"Good," Miss T. said. "Third grade teachers don't get anybody's attention."

Addie's memory of third grade reinforced that last statement and she laughed. They crossed the parking lot to the sidewalk and mingled with the crowds of people hurrying down the street. No one glanced twice at the old woman in the tattered scarf and Addie could see Miss T. relax.

They came to an underpass and Sam helped Miss T. down the steep concrete walk that tunnelled under Lake Shore Drive. Music drifted through the air and once in the tunnel, Addie saw where it was coming from.

An old black man with kinky grey hair, safe from the wind and the weather, leaned against the tunnel wall, playing the blues on an old, beat-up sax-ophone. The tips of the fingers on his worn-out gloves were cut off to make playing easier, but Addie could tell his hands were stiff with cold.

Miss T. approached him slowly, fumbling in her purse for something. The children saw her take out a 20-dollar bill and drop it in the hat that lay on the ground next to the man. His leathery face crinkled into a smile, though he kept on playing, and he nodded gratefully in Miss T.'s direction.

"What did you do that for?" Nick whispered loudly, once they were past the musician.

"That's the way he makes money," Miss T. answered. "I thought I'd help him out a little bit."

Nick wrinkled his nose. "Not much of a living."

"No, it's not," Miss T. sighed. "And I suppose I shouldn't have given him that much. He'll probably just go out and spend it on liquor at the end of the day."

Addie stared over her shoulder and Nick walked backwards, watching the old man and the people who dropped dimes and quarters into the hat. A couple of teenage boys entered the tunnel and the old man stooped swiftly to pick the twenty out of his hat and stuff it in his pocket.

Addie shivered, only partly from the cold. They came up the tunnel on the other side, directly in front of the John G. Shedd Aquarium. Since it was Thursday, admission was free to the original aquar-ium. But there had been another addition to the building, the Oceanarium, so Miss T. paid their entrance fees to that, and Nick and Addie raced ahead of the adults to the coral reef exhibit Addie had described earlier.

They were just in time to watch the diver feed the many varieties of fish, sharks, eels, and turtles that inhabited the tank. The sea turtle, a very large and very old fellow, followed the diver around, pushing his way to the bucket of food, bringing laughs from the hundreds of people who surrounded the tank.

Miss T. and Amy dawdled behind most of the afternoon, but Addie, Nick and Sam stayed together, examining the thousands of varieties of fish in smaller tanks situated in rooms that circled the coral reef. Addie was a little spooked by an octopus that hung overhead in one of the rooms, but Nick thought it was great.

The Oceanarium was even better. They watched dolphins perform gracefully in a large auditorium and saw beluga whales, sea otters, and seals through an underwater viewing window. In another exhibit penguins dove and zipped through the water at lightning speeds.

It was a long, lazy afternoon and they topped it off with an early supper at the aquarium's restaurant, Soundings. It was a beautiful restaurant with an expansive view of Lake Michigan. The sun had set and the city of Chicago was reflected in the lake.

Nick and Sam kept up a lively conversation, but Addie stared silently out the window, mesmerized by the lights dancing in the water. Miss T. interrupted her reverie.

"What are you dreaming about, miss?" she asked.

Addie smiled. "Not much. I was just thinking how—confusing Chicago is. I mean, there are so many opposites."

Nick arched an eyebrow and looked at Addie as if she were goofy. "What are you talking about?"

Addie blushed. "I'm not sure. But just think about what we've seen today. We're staying in a hotel suite that's probably worth more than my house. And yet there's a man in that tunnel playing the saxophone so people will give him their spare change."

She gestured toward the lakefront. "And look at all those boats out there. Those are just toys for the people who own them, but kids like Rico have to hustle strangers to help his mom provide for their family."

Nick shrugged. "So what can we do about it?"

When Addie smiled, Nick held up his hands in defense. "I know, I know. Don't tell me! Pray, right?"

Miss T. and Amy laughed, and Amy reached out to pat Addie's hand. "I think that's all the Lord would ask you to do right now, Addie. Maybe someday you can do more."

Miss T. nodded and asked, "Who's Rico?"

Addie and Nick told Miss T. about the boy they met that morning, and the old woman smiled at their vivid description of the scrappy little kid.

"I'd like to meet him," Miss T. said. "He sounds like my kind of people."

Addie and Nick both dozed in the car on the way back to Jean-Luc's. They didn't awaken until Sam bumped over the curb of the service drive at the hotel. He pulled around to the back and stopped by the big steel door.

But the door was locked and no amount of pounding seemed to attract the attention of anyone inside. Several people along the street were watching them and Miss T. began to get nervous.

"Someone needs to go inside and get the manager," she said.

"I'll go," Sam volunteered.

"No." Amy stopped him. "I'll go. You need to stay with Eunice and the children. I don't think anyone will bother you if there's a man here, but two old women and two children would be an easy target for a mugger."

"Oh, this was a stupid thing to do," Miss T. fretted.

"I'll hurry," Amy reassured her friend.

Addie stomped her feet and clapped her hands to keep warm in the cold December air. Although the area behind the hotel was deserted, there were noises in the alley and loud voices on the street. Addie glanced nervously around her and saw a shadow moving near the row of dumpsters at the very back of the lot.

There was the loud metallic crash of a dumpster lid being thrown open and Addie squealed. Miss T. put an arm around the girl and pulled her close.

"Shhh," Nick hissed loudly and Sam put a finger to his lips.

"It's just an old guy looking for food," he said quietly. "Don't pay any attention to him and he won't even know we're here."

They could hear the man muttering under his breath and Addie held hers.

"Nothing good here," he mumbled and his voice carried clearly across the empty lot. "What's this... chicken... hate their chicken... too greasy. Give me that milk!... What milk?... right there... don't drink milk, might make you sick. Can't get sick, big day tomorrow... got to go to work... can't go to work, you got fired." The wavery voice trailed off and they heard footsteps coming toward them.

The shadow grew larger and Addie could barely make out the bent form of an old man. She bit her lip to hold back tears of fright, and Nick took a deep breath and exhaled noisily. The footsteps stopped.

The man's face was still in the shadows, but Addie watched as his knarled old hand pulled a short knife out of his coat pocket. "Get out of my yard!" the old man yelled suddenly and Addie couldn't stop the cry that was choking her.

"Yo, Jack. It's me, Rico," said another, younger voice and Rico stepped from the shadows as well. Addie sagged against Miss T. in relief and the elderly woman swallowed hard.

"I'm headin' home, Jack. I just wanted to see how you was doing," the boy said. "Got enough to eat?"

"Never got enough," Jack muttered and slipped his knife back in his coat. "You got enough, Rico?"

"Always, Jack, always," Rico answered and pulled a large deli sandwich from inside his front pocket. "Here you go, old timer. Enjoy yourself, okay?"

"Okay, Rico, I will. Thanks, kid," the old man mumbled as he wolfed down the food.

The steel door suddenly yawned open and Amy appeared with Marcia.

"Come in, come in," Marcia exclaimed. "You must be freezing! I'm so sorry this happened, Miss Bryce. We were watching for you, but I had to answer a phone call, and the maid got called away to deliver some towels. I'm so sorry."

"Oh, hush, we're fine. Don't worry about us," Miss T. said. She glanced back at Rico and Jack, standing in the shadows. Addie and Nick waved to the boy and he lifted his hand in return.

"Who's that?" the old man asked. "Who's that, Rico? They got enough to eat?"

"Oh, yeah," Rico said softly. "They got enough, Jack."

"Here, Rico, give 'em some of mine," Jack said and pushed the remainder of the sandwich at his young friend.

"Sure, Jack, I'll give 'em some of yours," Rico said, and the steel door slammed shut.

Addie blinked back tears, Miss T. shook her head, and even Nick looked pale in the bright light of the corridor. Sam finally spoke.

"I think you're right, Addie. These people need prayer."

CHAPTER 7

More Missing Money

Marcia cleared her throat. "Uhm, I think we'd better get you to your suite, now."

"How's Rico going to get home?" Nick wanted to know. "It's dark out."

"Rico can take care of himself," Marcia assured him.

"But what about Jack?" Addie said.

Marcia sighed. "I'm sorry you had to see Jack," she said. "Jack is living the way he wants to live. We've given him jobs before and when he gets paid, he blows all the money on booze and doesn't show up again for a couple of weeks. What more can we do?"

"Where does he live?" Nick asked.

"On the streets. He's one of the vagrants they talk about every night on the news. I'm not sure the homeless problem is as bad as the media makes it, but they are there. If you're new to Chicago, it can be somewhat . . . disturbing when you see them for the first time. But after a while you adjust. You learn to live with it."

55

"Have you adjusted to Rico?" Addie asked softly.

Marcia glanced irritably at the young girl. "Rico is not homeless, and he's not an alcoholic," she said shortly. "There's a big difference."

Addie didn't answer and Miss T. spoke up. "Let's get upstairs. I could use some coffee."

Half-an-hour later, Nick was stretched out on the sofa in the sitting room and Addie was curled up in a big chair. Both of them were sipping steaming cups of hot chocolate while Sam sat on the floor and tossed marshmallows high in the air, catching them in his mouth.

The television was on, but no one was paying any attention to it. The basketball game was over and three different channels were playing the old movie *It's a Wonderful Life*. Addie clicked the remote and the television went dark.

"Hey," Nick protested, "I was watching that!"

"You've seen it a gazillion times, Nick," Addie said.

"Nothing better to do." He sighed. "Wish we had a good video to watch."

"Call room service," Sam suggested. "They'll send up a selection."

"How much would it cost?" Nick asked.

Sam laughed. "Not a dime. This is a classy hotel, and you've got Tierny Bryce in your suite. Nothing's too good for her. She's big time in this town."

Addie swung her legs down from the chair and paced up and down the room. "Doesn't this bother you at all?" she burst out. "Here we are, drinking hot chocolate and watching a big screen TV in a fancy hotel while that—that Jack is scrounging food out of dumpsters right outside our back door. And who knows what Rico's doing? He's probably not even home yet."

Sam and Nick exchanged glances, and Nick spoke quietly. "You heard Marcia, Addie. Jack's doing what he wants to do."

Addie shook her head. "I don't believe anybody would really want to live that way," she said.

"Of course not," Sam agreed. "He doesn't want to live *that* way, but he doesn't seem willing to try and live any other way, either."

"There's got to be a way to help him," Addie insisted.

Miss T. had entered the room and she heard the tail end of their conversation. She pulled Addie down on the sofa next to her. "Jack needs more help than we can give him in the few days we'll be here, Addie. And you know others have tried to help him. Until Jack wants to help himself, no one will be able to do much for him that will be very useful."

Sam nodded. "The best thing anyone could have done for Jack would have been to get hold of him when he was Rico's age, and shake some sense into him."

Addie's face brightened immediately. "Then that's what we can do! We can help Rico!"

Miss T. smiled at Addie's earnest young face. "We'll see, miss. I haven't really met the young man, yet."

"We'll find him tomorrow and introduce you," Addie promised. Then she yawned. "I think I better go to bed now," she said.

"It's only eight-thirty," Nick protested. "You can't be sleepy yet!"

"I've been awake since five," Addie informed him.

"What a party-pooper," Nick teased.

Addie stuck her tongue out at him and said good-night to everyone else. When she was ready for bed, Amy knocked softly on her door.

"Come in," Addie called.

"I hear you're conking out on us early tonight," Amy laughed. "Would you like to pray before you go to sleep?"

Addie nodded gratefully. "I always pray with my folks before bed," she said. "I kind of miss them."

Amy and Addie sat on the edge of the huge water bed and Amy prayed softly, thanking God for their safe trip and asking Him to give Addie wisdom in her desire to help Rico. Addie prayed for her parents and for the rest of their vacation time, and when they closed their prayer in Jesus' name, Addie could barely keep her eyes open. The gentle motion of the warm bed rocked her to sleep immediately.

* * *

Nick was in front of the television watching the news when Addie came out of her bedroom the next morning. He held up his hand for silence before she had a chance to speak.

" . . . and the reclusive movie star has not ventured far from her suite here at Jean-Luc's, an exclusive four-star hotel, since her arrival in Chicago yesterday morning."

"That's what you think," Nick laughed at the reporter.

"The word is she will remain here with her young friends, Addie McCormick and Nick Brady, until sometime tomorrow, when they have plans to dine with Miss Bryce's one-time costar and good friend, Winston Rinehart. Back to you, Carl."

"What?!" Nick shouted. "Winston's here?"

Miss T. stood in the door to her room and she frowned at the television. "No, he's not here yet, and that was supposed to be a surprise. Winston will be disappointed. Drat those nosy reporters."

"We'll act totally surprised," Nick told Miss T., and she winked at his smiling face.

"See that you do," she warned jokingly. "Now, come here and help me pick out my disguise for today."

Addie and Nick ran to her room and the three of them sorted through the bagful of scarves, hats, glasses, and wigs that Marcia had produced the day before. While they were searching for "just the right accessories," Nick joked, the door chimed.

"Come in," Miss T. called out and Addie heard a soft swish. Through the crack in the bedroom door, the children could see Carmen push another of the large white carts into the sitting room.

"Just leave it there, Carmen," Miss T. said through the door. "We'll set the table ourselves. We're not quite ready to eat."

"All right," Carmen called back and left quickly.

Today Miss T. was going to be a mousy brunette with furry earmuffs, and the same coat and glasses. They had just finished picking out the clothes when Addie heard the door slide open and shut once more. She waited to see who this was, but it was several seconds before Sam came in the room.

"Hi," Addie greeted him. "Where have you been so early this morning?"

Sam looked confused. "My bedroom. Why?"

Addie frowned. "I thought I heard the hall door open."

Sam shrugged. "You must have been hearing things. Wasn't me. What's on the agenda today?"

"Breakfast and then the Museum of Science and Industry," Miss T. said. "Let's eat."

Steaming croissants with lots of butter and strawberry jam were the highlight of Addie's breakfast, although there was plenty of sausage, bacon, eggs, juice, and fresh fruit as well.

When they were finished, everyone scattered to their assorted bedrooms to don coats, hats, and gloves. Sam and Nick came out of their room and Sam had a frown on his face.

"Anybody seen my billfold?" he asked.

Miss T. cocked her head toward the coffee table. "You left it over there last night."

Sam snapped his fingers. "That's right. I forgot." But when he crossed the room to get it, the coffee table held nothing but magazines and the vase of fresh flowers Carmen had brought with their breakfast.

"That's strange," Sam said. "No, wait a minute, here it is." He reached behind the table to the floor and picked up the black nylon billfold. He glanced quickly at its contents and frowned again. "What did I buy last night?" he asked the others.

No one could remember Sam making any purchases at all.

"Great," he sighed. "There's ten bucks missing. I know I had 25 dollars in here." He held up a single ten and a single five.

Addie spoke slowly. "And I never found my change purse yesterday. I set my purse on the sofa, but Nick found it on the floor. The zipper was open and my change was gone."

"You think somebody's stealing from us?" Nick asked.

Miss T. sighed and nodded. "Very likely. And it has to be one of the employees. They're the only ones who have access to these rooms. I suppose it's too great of a temptation to them when they see money laying around and no one in sight to stop them. I'll speak to Marcia about it."

"But why don't they take it all if they've got the chance?" Nick asked. "Addie had a lot more money in her purse than just that change. And Sam had 25 dollars. Why did the thief only take ten?"

"Because petty thiefs are smart," Amy said. "They steal small amounts in the hope that the people they steal from won't notice the difference. Or if they do, they'll blame themselves for misplacing the missing items, like Addie did yesterday."

"Well, let's not worry about it right now," Miss T. said. "I can give you both the money you've lost and I'm sure the hotel will reimburse me. Let's forget about it for today and enjoy ourselves."

They left the suite and headed down the long corridor toward the service room. But Addie hung back and Nick fell into step beside her.

"What's wrong?" he asked her. "You heard Miss T. She'll get your money back."

Addie shook her head. "I don't really care about that. It was only a dollar or two." She paused and Nick poked her in the side.

"Come on," he said. "Out with it."

She shrugged. "I don't know. I've got a feeling about this. I don't think the employees are stealing from us."

"Great," Nick moaned. "I know your feelings, and they always get us into trouble. There's nothing suspicious going on so just forget about it, okay, Addie?"

Addie made a face at him and said nothing. In her mind she could still see a white sneaker disappearing around the same corner they were now headed for. And she was convinced she had heard the door to the suite slide open and shut this morning, although no one was there.

No, something *was* going on and Addie was going to find out what it was.

CHAPTER 8

Narrow Escapes

The trip to the Museum of Science and Industry gave the children their first real taste of Chicago traffic. The museum was south on Lake Shore Drive. Unfortunately, a semitrailer carrying gasoline had jacknifed on the icy road early that morning and traffic was backed up due to the accident in the southbound lanes. By the time they reached their destination in the little car, everyone was stiff from the long ride.

"Finally," Nick grumbled as he unfolded his legs and got out of the back seat. "I hope this is worth it."

Sam looked at the young boy in surprise. "Have you been here before?" he asked Nick.

Nick shook his head and shrugged. "It's just a museum. They're all alike."

"Tell me that at the end of the day," Sam laughed.

They had arrived early, but lines were still long ("Christmas vacation," Sam said), and it took them several minutes to pay their entrance fees and hang up their jackets. Miss T. was reluctant to remove her coat and ear muffs, but the children assured her she still resembled an old school marm.

"I think we'd better split up," Miss T. said. "I was exhausted last night after trying to keep up with the three of you. Amy and I will take our time and we'll meet you for lunch. There's a place to eat downstairs. Let's meet outside the entrance at one o'clock."

That was fine with the children and they were gone before the words were hardly out of Miss T.'s mouth.

"What should we do first?" Nick asked, but he was immediately distracted by the wooly mammoth that stood at the entrance to "Earth Trek." So they toured that exhibit first and then went on to watch a baby chick hatch at the "Food for Life" exhibit.

Afterwards, Addie and Nick got into a heated discussion over whether to tour the "Coal Mine" or view the "Fairy Castle." Sam settled the argument by taking them through the "U-505 Submarine," a German vessel captured by the Navy during World War II. Then it was time for lunch and Addie and Nick were still arguing over which display to see next when they met Miss T. and Amy.

Everyone was starved and their sandwiches and drinks disappeared within minutes. Miss T. handed them each another ticket.

"You have to watch the movie that's playing in the Henry Crown Space Center," she insisted. "It's called *Ring of Fire*. All about volcanoes. I think you'll find it very interesting, but I especially wanted you to see that theater. You'll never forget it."

So Sam and the two children headed for the Omnimax Theater, and the experience was every bit as good as Miss T. had said. The theater was a huge domed structure. The movie screens wrapped around the room 180 degrees and overhead 180 degrees. Seats filled the other half of the room and were very comfortable. You almost laid on your back in order to see above you.

After the movie, they decided to wait in line for the simulated shuttle ride. Next, Addie finally convinced the two guys to view the "Fairy Castle." She was enthralled with all the miniature furniture and amazed by the fact that it was equipped with electricity as well as running water. But the boys were anxious to get to the "Coal Mine," so they left the castle and spent the remainder of the afternoon touring the mine and viewing the collection of vintage aircraft that hung overhead.

Miss T. and Amy were waiting on a bench near the entrance when Sam and the children finally joined them at five o'clock. Nick dropped to the floor next to Miss T. and rested his head against the bench.

"I think my brain is on overload," he sighed.

"I'm 'exhibited' out," Addie agreed.

Sam laughed. "So was it worth it?" he asked. "I mean, this is just a museum."

Nick's eyes were closed but he gave Sam a tired grin. "Definitely worth the ride here," he said. "It's even worth the ride back!"

"Which we need to start right now," Miss T. said. "It's already dark out, and I told Marcia we'd be

back by six so she'd be sure to have someone waiting for us."

It took a few minutes to find their coats. The area
was crowded with people headed for home, and
there was a lot of jostling and bumping elbows.
Miss T.'s ear muffs were the hardest to find. When
they were finally located, Addie frowned as the
elderly woman clamped them over her ears.

"I don't think those are yours, Miss T.," she said.

"They do feel tight," Miss T. agreed. "But who
else would wear these monstrosities?"

"Those are mine," said a soft voice at Miss T.'s
side. A little girl with curly blond hair and big
brown eyes was staring woefully at the elderly
woman.

"Are you sure, honey?" the girl's father asked.

"Yes, they must be," Miss T. said. "They're
much too tight for me." She tried to pull the muffs
off quickly and in her haste she caught a corner of
her wig and it came off too.

The little girl's eyes nearly popped out of her
head and then she began to giggle.

"Now, Heather," her father admonished her, but
he was grinning, and Nick and Addie had to turn
away to keep from bursting into laughter. Only
Amy seemed upset by the incident and she hurried
to help Miss T. replace the wig. While she was
pulling the inner cap down over her friend's head,
her arm brushed against the wire rim glasses that
were already too loose and they slid down Miss T.'s
nose and clattered to the floor.

The girl's father stooped quickly to pick them up.
"Here you go," he managed to say with a straight

face. "We'll get you back together before you—" He stopped abruptly and stared incredulously at Miss T., now with her wig on crooked and without eyeglasses. "Holy cow," he said softly.

"Connie, come here quick!" he called out, and a young woman, obviously his wife, joined them with another child in tow. "Are you who I think—" he began.

But his wife interrupted him with a muffled scream. "Tierny Bryce!" she cried out and immediately began digging in her purse and came out with a pencil and a scrap of paper. "I don't believe this! Can I have your autograph? Oh, please, you don't know what this means to me. I've always loved your movies and I was so excited to hear you'd be in Chicago! We're going to the opening next week—"

Despite Amy's pleas for quiet, the woman continued to babble and soon a crowd had gathered. Miss T. looked resigned and began to sign autographs.

Amy pulled Sam to one side. "Get the car and meet us out front. We've got to get out of here."

Addie and Nick went with him to the car and he parked as close to the entrance as he could get. It was several minutes before Miss T. and Amy appeared at the top of the steps and a crowd of people surrounded them. A guard from the museum was trying to help Miss T., but eager fans kept pushing paper and pencil at the woman and she scrawled hasty autographs on assorted scraps of paper before finally reaching the car.

Sam was a bolder driver than Willard had been and he pulled away from the museum so quickly people were scrambling to get out of his way.

"For heaven's sake, don't kill anyone!" Miss T. said sharply, but she breathed a sigh of relief when the last fan was left behind and they were on the road once more. Everyone was silent for several moments, then Nick reached over the seat to straighten the still-crooked wig and they all burst out laughing.

"Oh, dear," Miss T. finally sighed. "I suppose we were lucky to get away as easily as we did. But now we're going to be late."

Sam turned the radio on. "There should be a traffic report on WLS," he said. "We'll listen and see which is the quickest way back."

The report was far worse than anyone expected. The accident that had held them up that morning was compounded when the semi began to leak gasoline and workers were still trying to clean up the mess. The reporter estimated an hour travel time to downtown Chicago.

Sam frowned. "We don't have enough fuel to sit in traffic for an hour," he said.

"Is there another way back?" Miss T. asked.

Sam nodded slowly.

"Good," Miss T. said. "Let's take it."

Sam hesitated. "Lock your doors," was all he said.

It wasn't long before the rest of them realized the route they had to take to get back to the hotel was through a bad section of town. The streets were littered with trash and nearly every building had a broken window or two. Several were burned out, with crude graffiti spray-painted on the sides.

The night was cold, so there weren't many people out. But when Sam stopped at a red light, three teenage boys crossed the street in front of them. The last one slammed his hand down on the hood of the car and everyone inside jumped. That made the three boys laugh and one of them came back and began pounding on Sam's window, shouting obscenities. When he tried to open Sam's door, Miss T. spoke through gritted teeth.

"Can't you make a right turn on red?" she asked.

Sam peeled around the corner without hesitation, and Nick and Addie looked back to see all three boys shouting and making angry gestures at them.

No one spoke the rest of the way home, though everyone finally relaxed. Twenty minutes later, they pulled into the service drive at Jean-Luc's and the steel door opened before Sam had a chance to shut off the car.

"You're late," Marcia called out cheerfully. "No trouble, I hope?"

No one knew how to answer and finally Miss T. said, "No. No trouble."

"Strictly by the grace of God," Amy added.

CHAPTER 9

The Thief Returns

Marcia listened in silence to Sam's description of the mishap at the museum and their trip through the inner city. They had returned to their suite and everyone was in Miss T.'s bedroom, sitting around the table. When Sam finished, Marcia smiled ruefully at the somber faces around the table.

"Did you at least enjoy the museum?" she asked them.

"It was great!" Nick assured her.

"Yes, it was a very pleasant day," Miss T. added, "with a very unpleasant ending." The elderly woman looked pale and tired.

"I'm going to send up a pot of black coffee, some hot chocolate, and—" Marcia furrowed her brow, trying to decided what else to add. "Pizza," she finished triumphantly, "Chicago style. Deep pan, extra cheese, loaded with pepperoni and sausage and—"

"Black olives," Addie suggested.

"Mushrooms," Nick added.

Sam groaned. "You're driving me crazy," he said. "I'm starved. Being in mortal danger makes me hungry."

Everyone laughed, but Miss T. shook her head. "I'm just glad we're here, safe and sound, to laugh about it now."

Marcia agreed. "You were very lucky."

"Luck had nothing to do with it," Nick protested. "The minute I saw all those burned out buildings I started to pray."

Marcia looked a little startled but she smiled. "Well, don't stop now," she suggested. "If my guess is right, you'll be on the news tonight. I'm sure someone at the museum called the television stations. If you try to go out tomorrow there will be reporters watching every door in this place. And only prayer can protect you from those people!"

True to her word, Marcia had pizza delivered to their suite in less than half-an-hour. She helped Carmen roll in the cart herself and set the table in the master suite. Sam, Nick, and Addie tore into their meal. Miss T. and Amy proceeded more slowly, but it was only a matter of minutes before the pizza was history and Sam was stretching back in his chair with a satisfied sigh.

"What's for dessert?" Nick asked Marcia.

"You mean you're still hungry?" she laughed. "What would you like?"

Nick shrugged. "Not much. Got a candy bar?"

Marcia looked puzzled. "Of course," she said. "Haven't you found the snack food bar yet?"

"The what?"

"Come here," she said, and Nick, Addie, and Sam all followed her out to the sitting room. She opened a side door next to the television and revealed a small refrigerator. It was stocked with a variety of pop, candy bars, and chips as well as yogurt and fruit juices.

Nick's eyes lit up and he reached for a cola and two candy bars. Addie and Sam took one each.

"Miss T., do you want anything?" Addie called out.

"Pick me out a candy bar," Miss T. called back. "Amy, too."

Addie knew Miss T. liked chocolate and caramel, so she picked a bar that had both and got Amy a bag of chocolate-covered peanuts. Marcia went back to Miss T.'s room to clear the table and the children and Sam helped her clean up before eating their desserts.

Carmen came back for the cart and she and Marcia left together a few minutes later. Marcia paused just inside the door. "Would you like to watch a movie tonight?" she asked. "We've got quite a selection downstairs. I could pick out a few for you to choose from."

"That would be nice," Miss T. said. "You're very considerate, Marcia. Thank you."

Marcia winked. "It's my job," she said with a smile.

"Where's my candy bar, Addie?" Miss T. asked when the two women had left.

"On the coffee table," Addie answered. "Right. . here." Her voice trailed off in confusion. "They're gone."

"You probably left them in the frig," Sam said.

"No." Addie shook her head emphatically. "I know I set them down here."

Miss T. frowned, then glared at Nick out of the corner of her eye. "You're not hogging the candy, are you, Mr. Brady?"

"Of course not!" Nick protested, highly offended. "I already ate my two—okay, three," he confessed when Sam snickered. "But they weren't yours. I'll bet they're still in the frig."

So Addie opened the refrigerator once more. There was another chocolate and carmel bar inside, but it was tucked in the back, and there were no more bags of chocolate-covered peanuts.

"There's something going on," the young girl stated flatly. "I know I took those out and put them on the coffee table."

"So where are they now?" Nick sneered. "Did a ghost sneak in and steal them?"

"Hush, Nick," Miss T. said quietly. "Carmen was here. She brought the food up."

"But she was never in the room by herself," Addie pointed out.

Miss T. shook her head in frustration. "I don't know. I'll speak to Marcia about all of this when she comes back with the movies."

But Marcia was as puzzled as the rest of them about the candy's disappearance. She was even more upset to learn about the missing money.

"I just can't believe any of our employees would steal from you," she protested. "I know it occurs in many hotels, but immediate dismissal is the punishment here if anyone is caught stealing. And working at Jean-Luc's has a lot of prestige. Our employees know that. None of them would jeopardize their jobs with such behavior."

She looked around the room at the sober faces. "But the money is gone and the candy is missing," she admitted reluctantly. "I'll... check into this. And I'll make sure you're reimbursed for your losses. I'll bring the money back myself."

Marcia left and Addie, Nick, and Sam settled down to watch *Beethoven*, a canine caper with a St. Bernard as the star. It was a touching movie, but Addie had seen it once before and she dozed off long before the final scene.

She woke up to find Nick and Sam standing over her, tickling her nose with a cotton ball taped to the end of a straw.

"What are you doing?" she mumbled and reached up to brush the cotton ball away from her itching nose. She smeared her face with something white and sweet-smelling and began to sputter.

"You guys!" she cried, now fully awake. "What is this? Yuuuummmm," she finished, licking whip cream from the tips of her fingers.

Nick laughed gleefully and slapped Sam's outstretched palm. "Go look at yourself in the mirror, Addie!"

"Who cares what I look like?" she said calmly. "I love whipped cream. Where'd you get it, anyway?"

"Marcia had it," Nick confessed.

"I'll get her tomorrow," Addie said, "but I'll get you tonight!" She grabbed the can of whip cream from beside the sofa and squirted Nick full in the face. He yelped in surprise and tried to wrestle the can from her.

Miss T. emerged from her bedroom, clapping her hands sharply. "That's enough," she said and took the sticky can from the two children. "No food fights here, Mr. Brady," she said firmly.

"Addie started it," he said with an accusing laugh, and Addie swiped a glob of whip cream from his cheek and smeared it in his hair.

"I said enough!" There was just a hint of laughter in Miss T.'s voice. "Both of you, go shower and get ready for bed. Now," she commanded when Nick tried to grab the can from behind her back. They went reluctantly.

Addie was still thrilled with the luxury of a private bath and she took her time in the shower. The hot water never ran out like it did at home and there was no one to yell at her for steaming up the bathroom. When she finally emerged she was wrinkled as a prune. She brushed her teeth and combed out the tangles in her long black hair. Donning her robe, she rejoined the others just as the news began.

Sure enough, the top story on the nine o'clock news was the "sighting" of Tierny Bryce at Chicago's Museum of Science and Industry.

"... although Miss Bryce managed to slip away before the media could be contacted, we have with us tonight the family that first recognized the famed movie star."

Connie stood nervously next to the newsreporter, but she was still excited about her chance meeting with Tierny Bryce. She told the story of Miss T.'s "unveiling" and her daughter held up the ear muffs Miss T. had mistaken for her own.

"Just think Miss T.," Nick laughed, "you were done in by a pair of ear muffs."

"Hush," Miss T. said good-naturedly.

Several more people showed the reporter bits and pieces of paper Miss T. had signed for them. One man, desperate for an autograph, only had his paycheck. He proudly showed the reporter where Miss T. had signed the back of it.

"I didn't want to do that!" Miss T. sniffed. "But the man said it would be worth more with my signature on it than it would be in the bank. Some people!"

"...and so, Chicago, keep your eyes open. While Tierny Bryce is in town, it just might pay to help some little old lady across the street! This is Beverly LaForge for Channel Nine."

Sam began to laugh. "I can just see it. Every woman over 65 is going to be suspect tomorrow. Kids are going to be yanking at their hair and knocking off their glasses just to see if it's Tierny Bryce underneath a disguise!"

"Don't be silly," Miss T. said, but she looked a little worried.

The next story was about a drive-by shooting at Cabrini Green. Four teenagers had ridden by an apartment house and shot at three people coming out the entrance. A child had been critically wounded and his mother was in fair condition.

Nick sighed. "Back to reality. I don't want to watch this stuff. I'm going to go dry my hair." His hair was still wet from the shower and stuck out all over his head.

"Good idea," Addie teased. "You'll wake up looking like a porcupine if you don't."

He tossed a pillow at her and disappeared into his room. He was back in less than a minute with a very disgusted look on his face.

"You're not going to believe this," he said. "Someone's stolen my brush!"

CHAPTER 10

The Thief
Is Revealed

Miss T. studied the young boy. "Are you sure you brought it with you, Nick?"

Sam answered for him. "I know he did. I borrowed it this morning."

"Why don't you look for it again?" Miss T. suggested.

So Sam and Nick went back to their bedroom and made a thorough search, but the brush was nowhere to be found.

"This is ridiculous," Miss T. fumed. "Of course, I'm glad nothing of real value is being taken, but that's not the point. I'm afraid Marcia will have to see that Carmen is dismissed."

"How do you know it's Carmen?" Addie protested. The pretty Mexican woman with the quiet voice seemed incapable of stealing anything.

"Who else has been in here?" Miss T. replied. "Marcia told me Carmen had been assigned to our suite for the duration of our stay. I know she comes in to clean when we're gone. And she was the only one around when the other things disappeared."

Nick spoke up. "It's only a brush, Miss T. I'd hate to see her lose her job over a hairbrush. I don't mind looking like a porcupine for a couple of days," he tried to joke, but no one laughed.

"It's not just a hairbrush, Nick," Amy said. "Stealing becomes a habit that is very hard to break unless you're caught and punished for it. Most petty thiefs will tell you they can't break the habit on their own. Those who are caught almost always stop once they're punished."

"Even though Carmen will lose this job, she'll learn a lesson that will be more valuable in the long run," Miss T. said. "And I'm sure she'll find another job. I'll speak with Marcia again tomorrow."

Addie knew the subject was closed, so she said nothing more. When she went to her room to find Nick a hairbrush, he followed her.

"You still think it's not Carmen?" he asked her and she nodded silently. "Well, you better be able to prove your theory by tomorrow morning, or she's out of a job."

Addie handed him the brush and he left. Amy came in to say good night, and she and Addie prayed once more. But Amy could sense the girl's distress and she took Addie's hand.

"If you really believe Carmen is innocent," she told Addie, "pray and ask God to show us. He never wants to see the innocent punished unjustly."

Addie nodded and gave Amy a hug. "I will, Amy. Thanks. See you in the morning."

Amy left the room and turned out the light. The balcony curtains were drawn, but the bright lights of Chicago pierced through anyway and gave the room a soft glow. Addie had slept the first night with the bed curtains open, but tonight she pulled the cord and sheer pink curtains dropped all around her. She tried to relax in the gentle motion of the water bed, but to no avail. Sleep wouldn't come, so she prayed again for Carmen, and for the real thief. She prayed for her family, then her friends at church, and finally she prayed for all the kids in her classroom.

What's left to pray for? she thought. *All the missionaries around the world? Missionaries!*

Addie jumped from bed and found the letter from Katie and Taku in her coat pocket where she'd tucked it Thursday morning. They had been so busy seeing Chicago, she'd forgotten all about it. She flicked on the little brass lamp over her headboard, propped several pillows behind her, and settled down to read.

Katie and Taku had moved back to the States so Taku could go to school. Their little boys, Meren and Sunep, were adjusting well and enjoying preschool. Their baby daughter, Sentila, was having health problems. She had caught a respiratory virus, then developed bronchitis which led to pneumonia and six days in the hospital.

Poor Sentila, Addie thought. In her mind she could see the sweet little girl with the large dark eyes.

The next paragraph seemed to jump out at Addie. Katie and Taku had moved into student housing on the university campus and, "This is the first time our family has ever been privileged to inhabit more than one room—and it's wonderful!! . . ."

Addie finished the letter, then folded it carefully and put it back in the envelope. She gazed around the room at her luxurious surroundings and was a suddenly a little embarrassed at the wealth that was at her disposal. *Oh, don't think I'm not grateful for this opportunity, Lord. I am. I wouldn't have missed this for the world. Just help me to remember what real wealth is.* She turned off her light, rolled over, and fell asleep.

* * *

Morning came quickly and they were all gathered in the sitting room, watching cartoons and waiting for breakfast, when the door chimed. Everyone jumped, but no one moved to answer the door. No one wanted to face Carmen.

Finally Miss T. went to the door and jabbed the "open" button. Winston Rinehart stood in the doorway behind the familiar white breakfast cart. He and Miss T. embraced briefly, and Addie and Nick jumped up to greet their old friend.

"I commandeered this in the hallway," he laughed. "I told Carmen I'd do her job this morning."

"Good," Nick said emphatically and Miss T. gave Winston a brief explanation of their recent troubles.

Winston's black brows came together in a frown. "I would personally vouch for Carmen's integrity," he said forcefully. "I have patronized this establishment for many years and Carmen is one of the most trustworthy employees I have ever met. I would implore you to refrain from any hasty judgments in this matter."

Addie was immensely relieved to have Winston on her side and even Miss T. began to look a little doubtful.

"All right," the woman said. "I'll keep quiet for now. But if anything else turns up missing, I'll have to speak with Marcia."

"Good enough," Winston agreed. "Now for breakfast."

"Let's set up in my room," Miss T. suggested, so they wheeled the cart into the master suite and set the table quickly. Everyone sat down and Amy said the blessing.

Miss T. poured coffee for the adults, only to find they were short one cup. "Would you check the cart, Addie?" she asked. "See if there isn't one in there."

"Where?" Addie said. The cart was empty.

"Underneath," Winston told her. "They keep extra supplies in the cabinet below."

"That's right," Addie said, remembering the cleaning supplies she'd seen the night of their arrival.

She knelt next to the cart and opened the door. There were no cups there, so she went around to the other side. She opened that door and caught her breath.

"Any cups?" Miss T. asked.

"No—no cups," Addie managed to stammer. She returned to her seat and began eating.

Everyone else chatted amiably through breakfast, but Addie ate silently, staring at her plate most of the time. Nick glanced curiously at his friend once or twice, but said nothing.

Miss T. shared her coffee with Winston, and soon everyone was finished. Addie began clearing off the table.

"Thank you, dear," Winston said when Addie removed his empty plate.

"You're welcome," Addie said and poked Nick in the side. "Why don't you help?" she suggested.

Nick frowned, but began picking up juice glasses and silverware.

"Can Nick and I take the cart back to the kitchen?" Addie asked suddenly.

"Whatever for?" Miss T. said. "I'm sure Carmen will be here to get it in just a few minutes."

Addie shrugged. "I don't know. Something to do."

"We've got plenty to do today," Sam laughed, but Addie remained where she was, looking at Miss T.

"Well, I don't care, dear," said the woman. "Take it if you like. I'm sure you know the way by now. But come right back."

"Okay," Addie said and she finished clearing the table quickly. Together, she and Nick steered the heavy cart through the bedroom into the sitting room and out the door. Once they were in the hallway, Addie glanced behind her and started pushing the cart at a run.

"What's wrong with you?!" Nick complained, panting to keep up with her. "What's going on? You were acting strange all through breakfast."

"Wait till we get in the elevator," Addie said tersely.

The rolling cart was hard to stop, and they slid a little way past the door to the service room before bringing the cart to a standstill. They backed up and Addie held the door open while Nick maneuvered the cart through. Addie pushed the elevator button and the door sounded its customary "ping-pong" and opened. Nick pushed the cart straight in and the door shut behind them.

"Now what's going on?" Nick demanded.

Addied reached down and slid open the cabinet door on the breakfast cart. "Out," she said sternly.

Nick's mouth dropped open and his eyes nearly popped out of his head as he watched Rico untangle his legs and step out of the cart.

CHAPTER 11

"Where Did They Go?"

"You!" Nick sputtered angrily and for a second, Addie thought Nick was going to slug Rico. So did Rico, because he took a step back and curled his fist.

"I thought you were—were—" Nick was stuttering, he was so angry.

"We thought you were an honest kid," Addie said.

"Ain't no honest kids from my part of town," Rico spat out and stared at them defiantly. "You better let me outta here, too, or you'll be sorry."

"I can't believe you'd steal from us," Nick said.

Rico sneered. "Why not? What did I take that you need?"

"My hairbrush!" Nick sputtered.

"How many more you got at home?" Rico shot back and Nick didn't answer. "We ain't got *one*. And how much money did I leave in your purse?" he said to Addie. "An' in that wallet?"

Addie looked hard at the boy before she answered. "I know we've got a lot more money than you do,

Rico, but that's not the point. There are honest ways to get the things you need."

"Not for me, there ain't," he muttered.

The elevator came to a stop on the ground floor and the door began to open, but Addie reached over and pushed button seventeen. The door closed in the face of a very surprised bell boy.

"What are you doing?" Nick asked.

"We need to talk some more." To Rico she said, "There *are* ways. If nothing else, I would have given you the money."

"Yeah, right. Take pity on the poor street kid."

"You take money from the other people who come to this hotel!" Nick protested.

"I work for that money," Rico said.

Nick cocked an eyebrow and gave the boy a skeptical look. "How?"

A subtle change came over Rico and he grinned broadly at the two children. "Hey, dude!" he exclaimed and held out his hand, palm up. "When'd you hit town? Me and my brothers, we got a new act. You heard of the Jackson Five? Well, we're the Marzetti Five. Going all the way, man! Wait'll you see us in the big time. Just need some spare change to get us on our way. You can say you knew us when! Thanks, dude. I'll put ya in my memoirs!"

He dropped the act as suddenly as he'd started, and the sullen look returned to his dark eyes. "Makes rich white folks feel good about themselves to give a street rat like me their pocket change."

The elevator stopped on the seventeenth floor and Carmen's pretty face appeared as the door opened. This time Nick reached out and pushed "Ground level." Carmen's eyes widened in surprise as the door slid shut and the elevator began its descent.

"You must have heard us talking in Miss T.'s suite," Nick said. "Would you really let them fire Carmen instead of confessing what you did?"

Rico's bottom lip began to tremble and he swallowed hard. "Course not!" he protested. "But that old lady said she wouldn't tell if nutin' else disappeared so I wasn't gonna take any more stuff from your room."

"That's big of you," Nick muttered and Addie frowned at him.

"For all we know, Carmen could already be in trouble," she said. "Marcia was going to look into this. I think you need to tell her the truth."

"No way!" Rico protested. "She'll kick me out for good."

"I think you're wrong," Addie argued. "Marcia likes you. I'm sure she'd rather help you if you promise not to steal from any of the rooms again."

But Rico wasn't listening. "And don't snitch on me, either," he snarled, "or I'll—"

"You'll what?" Nick asked in a bored voice.

Rico was edging toward the elevator door and when they stopped at the ground floor for the second time, he managed to squeeze out before it opened very far. Marcia was waiting for them on the other side.

"Rico?" she said in surprise. "What's going on here? The maids told me Addie and Nick were riding the service elevator up and down, but I didn't know you were with them."

She stopped when she saw the fear in the young boy's expression and looked at Addie and Nick for an explanation. They said nothing, but Marcia saw the open cabinet door. Rico's Bulls hat was still inside and understanding dawned on her face. "Oh, Rico," she said sadly. Rico pulled himself out of her grasp and bolted for the door. No one tried to stop him and Marcia turned back to Addie and Nick with tears in her eyes.

"I think we need to talk," was all she said.

Marcia got in the elevator, and they all rode up to the seventeenth floor in silence.

Miss T. was waiting for them. She was surprised to see Marcia. "That took you quite a while," she said to the children. "Any trouble?"

Marcia nodded and tried to speak, but couldn't.

"We found the thief," Addie told her elderly friend.

"Who?"

"Rico," Nick said.

At first the name didn't register, but then Miss T. remembered. "You mean the boy you met when we arrived? The boy in the parking lot? How did you find out?"

Addie told Miss T. how she had discovered him in the breakfast cart that morning while looking for a coffee cup.

"Why didn't you say anything then?" Miss T. wanted to know.

Addie shrugged. "If you had known he was there, you would have had to turn him in. I wanted to give him a chance to do the right thing on his own."

Marcia finally spoke. "I've always trusted Rico. I guess my trust was misplaced."

"Maybe not." Miss T. was surprisingly understanding. "Have you had any other complaints since he's been around?"

"Oh, never about Rico. Our clients like him. There have been one or two cases of theft—like yours—but we never pursued them because the clients didn't think it was worth it."

Winston and Amy emerged from the master suite and Miss T. told them the news.

"You mean that urchin with the big eyes and the quick tongue?" Winston asked. Marcia nodded. "Well, I must admit he's talked me out of a dollar or two before, but I never imagined he would resort to theft."

Marcia sighed. "Rico's mom is alone and she has five mouths to feed. I'm sure Rico's capable of doing whatever it takes to put food on the table."

"Or a hairbrush in the bathroom," Nick said softly.

"What?" Winston asked, but Nick just shook his head.

"I told Rico we could work this out, if he promised never to steal again," Addie said to Marcia.

Marcia shook her head slowly. "I don't think so, Addie."

"But you've never had problems with the boy before," Miss T. said. "And I don't plan on pressing charges against him."

"What about all that talk of making a thief pay for what he's done?" Nick questioned his friend.

"Oh, I didn't say he wouldn't pay," Miss T. exclaimed. "I fully intend to make him work to pay back what he's taken. But Rico's still a very young boy, and he lives by the only rules he knows—how to survive on the streets of Chicago. It wouldn't be fair to judge him too harshly until he knows there are different rules."

"Please give him another chance, Marcia," Addie begged. The woman shook her head and Addie was desperate to change her mind. "You said yourself the clients like him. And I know *you* like him. Just one more chance. Put him on probation. He has to stay out of the service area and if there are any complaints from anyone he has to go."

"Addie, Addie," Marcia said and took the young girl's hand to stop her frantic appeal. "I'd love to give Rico another chance. I agree with everything that's been said. But I *know* Rico. He's very proud. He despises anything that resembles pity." Marcia sighed. "He won't be back," she said gently.

Suddenly, in her heart, Addie knew Marcia was right and she swallowed hard. The room was silent and Marcia stood to go. She and Miss T. spoke quietly at the door, and then she was gone.

Miss T. came back and gave Addie a long hug. "We've already talked about this, miss," the woman said. "It's very difficult to help people who don't want to be helped."

"I know," Addie said.

"So, let's put this behind us. You still have two days in Chicago," Miss T. said. "What do you want to do today?"

"Actually," Winston interrupted, "I was hoping to take you on a personal tour."

Addie and Nick both brightened considerably, but Miss T. was apologetic.

"Would you mind if I stayed in, Winston?" she asked. "I was going to let Sam chaperone while I rested. But I'm sure none of them will object if you lead the excursion today."

"We'd love it," Addie said, and Sam and Nick agreed.

"Good," Winston smiled. "And no, I don't mind if you rest. I'm sure your adventures yesterday would have worn *me* to a frazzle. So you relax," he instructed Miss T. "And you dress warm," he told the children.

"Where are we going?" Addie asked.

"You can't visit Chicago without walking the 'Magnificent Mile,'" he said.

"Where is it?"

"You're standing on it," he laughed. "Michigan Avenue has some of the most beautiful and famous architecture in the world."

"Won't people mob you like they did Miss T. yesterday?" Addie was hesitant to walk about Chicago with another famous person.

"Oh, no," Winston laughed. "I'm quite a familiar face anymore. I come to Chicago often so people are used to me. And of course, I didn't disappear for 45 years, either."

"That probably helps," Miss T. said dryly.

Addie, Nick, and Sam bundled up in scarves, hats, and mittens, and the four of them left soon afterward. Since their hotel was on the north end of Michigan Avenue, they walked south and Winston gave them brief but informative lectures on many of the buildings they passed.

Addie was most interested in the Water Tower. One of the few buildings to escape the Great Fire of 1871, its Gothic structure stood out among the more modern skyscrapers like the John Hancock Building.

Nick liked the Tribune Tower. He was impressed by the fact that many of the small stones at its base were taken from such famous buildings as the Westminster Abbey and the Taj Mahal.

Winston enjoyed sharing all he knew with them and they were able to walk freely in the streets. Although people recognized the elegant old gentleman, requests for autographs were scarce and no one followed them. They walked all the way to the Wrigley Building before lunch.

"My goodness, it's after one o'clock," Winston exclaimed. "No wonder I'm so hungry. Why don't we walk back to Water Tower Place and eat lunch there?"

"Is that the shopping complex?" Addie asked.

Winston nodded. "Maybe you can look for souvenirs before we go back to the hotel."

A brisk walk back up Michigan Avenue got them to their destination quickly, and burgers and fries filled their hungry stomachs. The shopping complex was seven stories tall and they spent the better part of the afternoon browsing through the countless stores and boutiques constructed around a grand atrium. Nick made several purchases—mostly sports paraphernalia with the Chicago Bulls plastered all over everything—and together he and Addie got a postcard to send to Brian.

Addie bought a miniature pewter replica of the Water Tower and she was still agonizing over whether to buy her mother a very expensive pair of earrings at Marshall Field & Company when they called it quits at five o'clock.

"Buy them, Addie," Nick finally said. "If you don't, we'll hear about it for the rest of the weekend."

"Okay," she said, "if you'll come with me."

Winston sat down on a long bench. "Sam and I will wait right here. Don't get lost."

"We won't," Addie assured him, and the two children ran into the large department store. But the jewelry department was not where Addie thought it was and they spent 15 minutes searching for it. When they finally found it, it took another ten minutes to find the pair of earrings Addie had selected earlier. By the time the purchase was made, it was close to five-thirty.

"Come on, Addie," Nick urged her when she stopped to look at a necklace that matched the earrings. "We've been gone too long already." They hurried down the escalator to the first floor and left the department store.

Nick stopped short. "Where did they go?"

Addie looked around her in confusion. Winston and Sam were nowhere in sight.

CHAPTER 12

Water Tower Place

Addie panicked for a brief moment and a big lump formed in her throat. But she swallowed the lump and forced herself to think. When she did, logic took over.

"We came out of the store on the wrong side of the mall," she told Nick. She pointed to the glass elevator in the center of the atrium. "We're in the center of the mall. Winston and Sam are waiting at the entrance by the street."

Nick shook his head vehemently. "They were waiting right on that bench," he said, pointing to a bench near the elevator.

"No," Addie argued, "Winston and I sat there and waited for you and Sam when you went to buy your Bulls cap. Now he and Sam are waiting on the other side of the mall. We have to go back through Marshall Field's and find the street entrance."

"Are you sure?" Nick asked.

Addie nodded confidently, so Nick followed her back through the department store and out the other side. But Winston and Sam weren't there either.

Addie's forehead puckered in a worried frown. "I *know* this is where they sat down," she exclaimed. "Don't say 'I told you so,'" she warned Nick. She could tell the words were ready to jump right out of his mouth.

He shrugged. "So where are they?"

Addie glanced at her watch. "We've been gone for 45 minutes. I imagine they're looking for us. They probably think we're lost."

Nick sniffed. "They're right."

"We're not lost!" Addie insisted.

"What? They are?" Nick said sarcastically.

"They're not where they're supposed to be!" Addie retorted.

"How can you be sure this is where they're supposed to be?" Nick shot back.

"Because this is where we left them!"

"But they're not here!"

"Okay, okay." Addie took a deep breath. "Let's just calm down and stop yelling. People are looking at us." She thought hard for several moments. "We have to start somewhere, so let's just agree for the time being that this is where we left them, okay?"

Nick nodded reluctantly.

"When we didn't come back right away, they probably went into Marshall Field's to the jewelry department to find us. Let's go back and see if they've been there."

Nick rolled his eyes, but he followed Addie through the famous department store for the third time that day. When they reached the jewelry counter, the woman who had waited on them smiled and spoke first.

"Your friends were looking for you," she said.

Addie gave Nick a tiny smirk and he made a face at her.

"But I thought you went that direction so that's where I sent them." The sales clerk pointed toward the center of the mall.

"Thanks," Addie said. "We'll find them."

They hurried through the store and came out near the glass elevator. No Winston or Sam.

"Great," Nick moaned. "You suppose they went back to where we started?"

Addie was discouraged. "Probably," she said. So they trudged back through the store to their original meeting place but no one was there.

"You know," Nick said, "we're probably chasing each other around this stupid place. I say we sit here and wait. They've got to show up sometime."

They were still sitting at six-thirty. Finally Addie stood up. "I didn't want to do this," she said, "but I think we need to call the hotel."

Nick made a face, but he nodded. "Come rescue us," he said in a whiny voice. "We're lost!"

Addie giggled. "I feel kind of stupid," she agreed.

They found a pay phone, pooled their change, and got the number of Jean-Luc's from the operator. When the person at the desk answered, Addie asked to be connected to Tierny Bryce's suite.

"Who's calling please?" the voice said.

"It's Addie," the girl answered. "She'll know who I am."

The voice sighed. "Is this the same Addie who called five minutes ago? Or are you the Addie that called this morning?"

"What?" the young girl asked. "I haven't called at all. What are you talking about?"

"What's going on?" Nick whispered. He pulled Addie and the receiver close to his ear so he could hear too.

"Miss Bryce has received a number of calls from 'Addie' today. Unless you have more information that would indicate you're who you say you are, I'm afraid I have to refuse your call."

Addie and Nick exchanged a frustrated glance. "What kind of information?" she asked.

"Miss Bryce's room number or a—"

"She doesn't have a room number," Nick muttered. "She doesn't even have a door knob."

Addie giggled and the voice laughed, too. "Now that's what I needed to hear. Just a moment, please." There was a slight pause and then the phone began to ring in Miss T.'s suite.

"Thank You, Lord," Addie whispered and Nick said, "Amen."

But no one answered the phone and the voice came back on the line. "I'm sorry, Miss Bryce is not in her room."

"Or she's got her hearing aid out," Nick whispered.

"Could we leave a message?" Addie asked.

"Of course. What would you like me to tell her?"

"Um..." Addie took a deep breath and finally admitted, "We're lost."

"What?" Now the voice sounded concerned.

"Well, we're not lost exactly," Addie said hastily. "We know where *we* are, we just don't know where... anyone else is."

There was a moment's silence and Addie was positive she could hear the voice smile. Then it asked, "Where are you?"

"We're at Water Tower Place," she replied.

"All right," the voice answered. "Why don't you go to the glass elevator on the ground floor and wait there? We'll send someone down to get you right away."

"Well," Addie hesitated. "I think Winston and Sam are still here, looking for us. Have they called you yet?"

"No." The voice was confused.

"We came with Winston Rinehart and our friend, Sam, but we got separated," Addie explained. "I'd hate to leave before we found them. But I thought maybe they had called to see if we had called—oh, this is getting confusing."

The voice agreed. "I'm not sure what to do. Who's been your assistant here at the hotel?" she asked.

"Marcia Vetter," Addie said.

"Fine. I'll page Marcia and send her to Water Tower Place to find you. The three of you can take it from there."

"Thank you," Addie said gratefully. "We'll be on the first floor by the elevator. Goodbye." She hung the phone up and picked up her packages.

"Marcia's coming," she said, although Nick had heard the whole conversation.

"Yeah," he said with some disgust. "Marcia's coming to rescue the little country hicks who can't find their way out of the mall."

Addie grinned. "I don't care," she said. "I'll just be glad to get back to the hotel. I hope we can find Winston and Sam. I'm starved."

"So let's eat," Nick said.

They bought more burgers and fries at the same restaurant they'd stopped at for lunch. They ordered them to go, and sat on the bench near the elevator, munching in silence. Suddenly, Addie choked on her sandwich and swallowed quickly. She poked Nick in the side.

"Look," she whispered, although there was no one near enough to hear her.

She pointed to their right and up one level to the balcony above. Rico leaned against the rail, talking with a well-dressed man.

"Working for his money," Nick grumbled.

But Rico and the man seemed to be in a serious discussion and there was no evidence of the cocky street kid in Rico's behavior. Instead, he shook his head several times and frowned. They finally came to some sort of agreement and the man reached in his jacket and gave Rico several bills.

Rico pocketed the money and removed a small package from his coat. It was wrapped in plain brown paper and they made the exchange quickly. The man tried to be discreet, but Addie could see his eyes scan the area before he turned to leave.

Rico stayed where he was until the man was gone. Then he slipped the bills from his pocket, counted them once and put them back. He sauntered to the escalator and ran lightly down the moving stairs.

When he reached the bottom he turned toward Addie and Nick, seeming to sense someone was watching him. The two children stiffened automatically and Rico caught sight of them. They stared at one another for several moments. The sullen look returned to Rico's face and he backed up slowly, then turned and hurried from the mall. The light-hearted bounce was gone from his step.

Addie and Nick were too startled to say anything for a long moment. Then Nick released the breath he had been holding and looked at Addie. The sick feeling she had in the pit of her stomach was mirrored in his eyes.

"Marcia said he had other jobs."

Addie nodded. "Maybe it's not—what it looks like."

"Don't kid yourself, Addie," Nick said bluntly. "A kid like Rico is—"

"There you are," said a voice from behind them and they both jumped. Marcia stood smiling at them. "What's the scoop? Where are Winston and Sam?" she asked.

Just as Addie opened her mouth to tell Marcia their story, she spotted Winston and Sam hurrying down the escalator, two steps at a time. The old gentleman had a hard time keeping up with Sam, but he slowed to a walk when he saw the children and Marcia standing by the elevator.

"Thank heaven," he said, breathing heavily. "I was so afraid something had happened to you both."

"I tried to tell him not to worry," Sam grinned. "I figured you'd have enough brains to find a telephone—even if you couldn't find your way out of Marshall Field's!"

Nick groaned. "I knew we'd never hear the end of this from you," he said.

"Maybe next time we go out we should get a couple of those leashes moms put on their little kids," the older boy teased them.

Addie poked Sam good-naturedly. "Oh, hush," she said, sounding remarkably like Miss T. "I don't care how much you tease us. I just want to get back to the hotel. I'm tired of walking."

"I've got a limo waiting outside," Marcia said. "I'm certainly glad nothing serious happened," she added.

Neither Nick nor Addie replied and she studied the two carefully. "Nothing serious did happen, did it?"

Addie managed to smile and shake her head. "No," she said. "Nothing happened."

They walked out of Water Tower Place to the waiting limo, but Addie and Nick were strangely quiet all the way back to the hotel.

CHAPTER 13

By Invitation Only

"It was entirely my fault," Winston kept repeating to Miss T. once they were back at the hotel. "Entirely my fault. I should never have let them go by themselves."

Miss T. put a gentle hand on the old man's arm, but she spoke bluntly. "Frankly, Winston, you're the only one still upset about all of this. Nothing happened. The children are fine. Stop worrying!"

Winston nodded and sipped his coffee. They were seated around Miss T.'s table, eating a light supper. Addie and Nick were nibbling at their sandwiches and Amy urged them to eat.

"You must be hungry after your ordeal," she said.

"We stopped at the restaurant where we ate lunch and got something to eat," Nick admitted.

Sam reached a long arm across the table and grabbed Nick's sandwich from his plate. "You mean we were scouring the mall for you two and you were stuffing your faces with burgers and fries?" he exclaimed between bites.

Everyone laughed and Nick grinned sheepishly. "Nothing else to do," he said.

Winston smiled at the joking children, but he leaned toward Miss T. and whispered loudly, "I'm getting too old for this, Tee."

"No, you're not," Miss T. said with a wink at Addie. "Beat you to it, miss," she said and Addie grinned.

Nick slurped the rest of his soda and stretched back in his chair. "Can I be excused?" he asked in a tired voice. "I'd like to tube out tonight, if no one cares."

Miss T. smiled fondly at the young boy. "Go ahead, dear. You're all excused, if you like."

Addie and Sam followed Nick into the sitting room. Addie flopped onto the sofa and Sam opened the wall cabinet and clicked on the large screen TV Nick pulled one of the pillows from underneath Addie's head and tossed it to the floor.

"Ouch," Addie said halfheartedly.

"If you're going to hog the sofa, you've got to share the pillows," Nick said.

"Yeah," Sam agreed and pulled out another one. He glanced back at the adults in Miss T.'s room and adjusted the volume on the television. He found a boring news channel and tossed the remote on the coffee table.

"Now." Sam looked from Addie to Nick. "The truth. What happened at the mall today?"

The children exchanged a brief glance and Nick sighed. Addie told Sam about their chance meeting with Rico and he shook his head sadly.

"Kids like Rico don't get much of a break," Sam said. "Drugs are quick, easy money if you don't get caught."

"We don't know for sure it was drugs," Addie insisted.

"Come on, Addie," Nick said. "Get real. A brown paper package about so big," he gestured with his hands, "worth a lot of money. What do you think it was?"

"I don't know." Addie blinked back quick tears and closed her eyes. "I don't want to think about it."

Sam picked up the remote and found another station with a bad movie on it. They watched in silence until the next commercial. Winston and Miss T. came into the room. Winston was leaving and Addie sat up to tell him goodbye.

"Will we see you again?" she asked.

"Oh, yes," Winston replied. "We're all going to the ribbon cutting ceremony tomorrow afternoon."

"Would you like to go to church with us?" Amy asked.

"We're going to church?" Nick was surprised. "Where are we going? That big cathedral across the street from Water Tower Place?"

Amy shook her head. "No. Sam is taking us to his church. It's more like our church at home."

"Good." Addie was relieved. Fancy cathedrals were nice to look at, but pretty overwhelming. She'd been overwhelmed by enough things in Chicago already. She wanted to worship somewhere she could relax.

Winston shook his head. "I'm afraid I have other commitments," he said. "Thank you anyway." He left and they went back to their movie. But it was really very bad and everyone was tired. They decided to go to bed early in preparation for church the next morning.

* * *

Sam's church was indeed like their church at home, and Addie was comfortable right away. The building was small and the sanctuary was an intimate place. This service was a little more structured and they used a small pipe organ instead of instruments, but Addie enjoyed listening to the prayer requests of the various members. And the text for the message seemed to speak directly to her heart.

" 'For I know the plans I have for you,' declares the Lord, 'plans to prosper you and not to harm you, plans to give you a future and a hope.'" It was a passage from Jeremiah and it seemed particularly appropriate to Addie that morning.

As tired as she was, she had laid in bed for quite a while the night before, going over the scene in the mall and praying for Rico. Now, as she listened to the minister speak, her thoughts began to wander.

Did God have "a future and a hope" for Rico? Of course He did. God's promises were for everyone— everyone who believed in Him, anyway. Did Rico believe in Him? Addie wasn't sure, but she doubted it. Had Rico even heard of Jesus? There was no way of knowing and she sighed deeply. Miss T. glanced at her and Addie forced herself to concentrate on the message, but not before she thanked God once more that He was in control of things.

No one mobbed Miss T. after the service, although many people stopped to say hello and welcome them to Chicago. They lingered there for half-an-hour, talking with Sam and Amy's family. When they finally arrived back at the hotel, everyone was hungry.

"Don't eat very much," Miss T. warned them. "There's a buffet after the ribbon-cutting ceremony—around two o'clock, I think. And the food will be delicious, so save your appetites."

"I thought we were eating at some banquet tonight, where you're supposed to be the guest speaker," Nick said.

Miss T. nodded. "We are. That's at seven o'clock."

Nick puffed out his cheeks and held his arms out in front of his stomach. "Fat city," he said.

Miss T. sniffed. "That's the least of your problems," she said. "Only us old folks have to worry about that."

So they snacked on a huge plate of nachos and cheese and after they were finished, Miss T. sent them to their rooms to change.

"What do you mean, dress up?" Nick protested. "This is dressy." He was wearing good slacks and a sweater.

"Suit and tie, Mr. Brady," Miss T. said firmly. Nick sighed and followed Sam into their bedroom.

Addie changed into a black skirt with a red jacket and a white blouse, and Miss T. smiled at the young girl approvingly when she emerged from her bedroom, teetering just a bit on the low black heels her mother let her borrow.

"Very nice, miss," the elderly woman said. She was dressed in a floor-length black gown with a simple gold belt. Her grey hair was pulled back in a bun with a shiny gold clasp. She wore a single strand of pearls and a touch of makeup. Addie was impressed.

So was Nick. He whistled loudly when he joined them in the sitting room. He and Sam both wore dark suits and ties. Nick's tie was a little crooked so Miss T. straightened it. Amy also wore a floor length gown that was silver and grey.

"We're a pretty classy looking bunch, aren't we?" Sam grinned.

Miss T. nodded. "I just hope this is worth it," she said under her breath, but Nick heard her and looked at her in surprise. "I don't like getting dressed up any more than you do," she admitted with a laugh.

For the first time since they had arrived, they all left the hotel through the front door. Addie barely had time to take in the marble floors, the oversized plush furniture, and a virtual jungle of hanging plants and small potted trees in the lobby before they were whisked out the huge glass doors to the white limousine. A crowd had gathered and they cheered loudly when Miss T. came out. She smiled and waved briefly, and then they were gone.

The Kensington Center for the Performing Arts was only a few blocks south of their hotel, off Michigan Avenue on Chestnut Street. Winston arrived in a black limo directly ahead of them. There was a crowd here as well, and they roared their approval when Miss T. and Winston joined arms and entered the immense building.

Cameras whirred and clicked and dozens of reporters stood behind the heavy gold ropes that kept the crowd back from the wide sidewalk. Addie and Nick, then Amy and Sam followed the elderly couple into the center.

Inside, the lobby was brightly lit and lined with tables full of food. Nick sniffed at the mouthwatering aromas drifting through the room and Addie poked him.

"Control yourself," she teased him. "I can hear you salivating."

"I'm starved," Nick hissed back.

Amy fell into step with Nick. "The ribbon cutting ceremony won't take long," she murmured. "Then you'll be free to snack for the rest of the afternoon."

The ceremony took longer than anyone expected, of course. First the director of the center had to make a speech and then the president of the Chicago chapter of the actor's guild spoke. Finally, the mayor gave Miss T. and Winston keys to the city and then they both held onto a giant pair of scissors and snipped the ribbon.

"Finally," Nick muttered. "Can we eat now?"

A waiter dressed in a fancy tuxedo showed Miss T. and Winston to the beginning of the food line and the children followed them. They filled their plates with tiny sandwiches and fancy breads and dips and chips of all kinds. They returned to the head table at one end of the room and Nick dug in at once.

Addie ate slowly, more interested in watching the people around her. The lobby was filled with hundreds of people, all of them exquisitely dressed.

"Are these the same people who were waiting outside?" she asked Sam.

"Oh, no," he shook his head. "These are Chicago's elite. The people outside are just spectators. The exhibit won't open to the public until tomorrow. This is an exclusive event," he said in a haughty voice and crooked his little finger. Addie laughed.

"How did these people get in?" Nick asked. "Couldn't you just get real dressed up and walk in the front door?"

"Not without an invitation," Sam said.

"We didn't have an invitation," Nick persisted.

Addie rolled her eyes. "We didn't need one, goofus," she said and inclined her head toward Miss T.

Nick blushed and grinned. "Yeah, I guess not," he admitted. He leaned around Amy and caught Miss T.'s eye. "Can we have seconds?" he whispered loudly. Everyone at the table laughed and Miss T. nodded.

"Come on," he said and pulled at Addie's elbow. "I want some more of those little crescent rolls filled with the shrimp salad."

"Me too," Sam said. The three of them returned to the food tables and filled their plates once more.

"Where are those chocolate pudding cups you were eating?" Addie asked Nick.

Nick turned and pointed to a table across the room, but his eyes widened in shock and Addie followed his gaze. Then she turned back to Sam.

"Are you sure this is an invitation-only event?" she asked skeptically.

Sam nodded. "Why?"

Addie pointed to a small boy in a brown suit. His pant legs were too short and white socks showed conpicuously above dirty white sneakers. His black hair was plastered to his head and his tie clashed with his shirt.

Sam's mouth dropped open and they all watched in amazed silence as Rico piled a plate high with food, then casually began slipping tiny sandwiches into the frayed pockets of his worn jacket.

CHAPTER 14

Even Up

Another tuxedoed waiter spotted Rico about the same time Nick did, and he bore down on the small boy with a frown on his face.

Nick reached over and pushed half-a-dozen forks off the serving table they were standing near. They clattered to the floor and made a tremendous noise. Rico looked up and saw the waiter approaching him. He moved quickly into the crowd of people and the waiter had a difficult time keeping up with him.

Nick stooped over and picked up the forks. They watched the man pursue Rico across the room, dodging well-dressed couples and other waiters carrying trays full of drinks. Rico finally won out when an unusually large woman stopped the man in pursuit, insisting on service of some kind. Addie watched the boy slip through a swinging door and disappear.

"Good," Sam said. "He got away." He shook his head in disbelief. "That kid must have connections all over town." He turned to Addie and Nick. "Come on," he said suddenly.

Sam led the two children across the room and through the swinging doors. They found themselves in a long narrow hallway with doors on either side.

"What are we doing?" Nick wanted to know.

Sam grinned sheepishly. "I'm not sure," he admitted. "Let's see if we can't find Rico."

They spread out down the hall, trying to glance casually through the glass windows that were at eye level on every door.

"Pssst," Addie hissed softly. The fourth door on the right proved to be the magic one. Rico had jumped up on a long table full of napkins, table cloths, and other assorted linens. He was sitting there, swinging his legs and talking to a man who was folding something large and white. The three of them could just make out the conversation on the other side of the door.

"Thanks, Joey," Rico was saying. "This is good stuff." He stuffed a small sandwich in his mouth and the man laughed.

" 'S okay, Rico," Joey replied. "You take care of me, I take care of you." He patted something on the table and Addie saw another small brown paper package. "How's Gina?" the man asked.

Rico shrugged. "Ma's tired," he said. "Ma's always tired."

Joey nodded sympathetically. "Your ma, she works hard, Rico. You help her, you hear me?"

"Hey, I'm helping, I'm helping," Rico said with a gesture at the package and Joey laughed. "Gotta go,

Joey. The little kids are waiting for me. See you around."

"Yeah, see ya, Rico."

Rico jumped off the table and started to leave, but another man stopped him and they began to talk.

"Stay here," Sam whispered. "I'll be back in a flash."

"Now what?" Nick muttered, but they stayed where they were and continued to watch Rico, although they couldn't hear his conversation.

True to his word, Sam was back in a couple of minutes. He was pulling on his coat with one hand and carrying Nick's and Addie's. "I told Amy we were bored so we're going for a walk. Has he left yet?"

"No," Addie whispered. "What's the point, Sam? What are we going to do? Rico doesn't want to talk to us."

"He doesn't have to," Sam whispered back. "I just want to see some things for myself."

Rico finished his conversation with the man and disappeared around a corner.

"Let's go," Sam said. He stopped whispering and strode boldly through the swinging door.

Joey turned around and frowned at the three strangers walking through his laundry. "Who are you?" he demanded.

"Hi, Joey," Sam said. "We're friends of Rico. He go this way?"

Joey nodded, still suspicious, but he let them pass. They turned the corner after Rico and came upon a big metal door marked EXIT. Sam opened it slowly. They were in an alley behind the center.

"Are you game?" Sam asked the two children in a low voice. They both nodded. "Okay, let's go."

They followed Rico at a safe distance and crossed Michigan Avenue. Soon they had crossed the river as well and the streets began to grow narrow, the buildings got smaller, and the people began to change. The well-dressed upper-class men and women in their wool coats and leather jackets changed to working-class men and women in nylon coats and heavy boots. Rico seemed to know them all.

He came to stop in front of a small laundry and dry-cleaning establishment. It was a run-down building with a neon light that said MARZETTI CLEANERS. He breezed through the front door and past the counter.

Sam and the children stayed back on the street. They could see clearly inside the glass window front and watched Rico talk briefly with a man inside, then disappear through a door to the back.

"Got anything you need dry-cleaned?" Nick asked sarcastically, but Sam ignored him. Then the older boy pointed to the second story. Rico was framed in a window above them. Two smaller, black-haired boys were jumping up and down in front of him, and Addie could see him hand them food from the plate he'd been carrying. He would tease them by holding the food above their reach, and they took turns pulling on his arms and punching him in the stomach.

A woman appeared in the window, and she put an arm around Rico's shoulders and kissed the top of his head. Rico kissed her cheek and continued handing out food.

Addie sighed. "He lives above a laundry."

Nick shrugged. "It's not as bad as I thought it would be," he said.

Sam agreed. "This isn't the best part of town, but it's not the worst, either," he said.

Addie thought of the huge country house she lived in with her parents. The apartment above the laundry would probably fit in their living and dining rooms combined.

"Let's head back," Sam said. "It's getting late. I know I said this wasn't the worst part of town, but I don't want to get caught here after dark."

"It's almost dark now," Addie said.

Sam nodded. "Can you walk *real* fast in those heels?" he asked.

Nick was still watching the scene in the window. He saw his friends deserting him and hurried to catch up with them. He kicked a can off the middle of the sidewalk and a dog trotted out from behind a shoe repair shop and began barking.

Addie looked back. The dog was following Nick and growling. Nick kept glancing over his shoulder and he shouted at the mutt.

"Get outta here! Go on, leave me alone."

Sam kept walking but he spoke calmly over his shoulder, "Quiet, Nick. You're just antagonizing him. Act like he's not there and he'll probably leave you alone."

So Nick stared straight ahead and caught up with his friends. The dog trailed behind them for the next block, then abruptly stopped barking and went home.

They all breathed a sigh of relief, but they kept up their brisk pace. Night was falling quickly and street lights were coming on all around them. Sam led them back through the maze of streets. He seemed to know exactly where they were going and neither of the children thought to question him.

"Just about there," Sam said and turned a corner around a tall building.

Four teenage boys turned the corner from the other direction and the two groups almost collided. One of them obviously thought Nick was a little too close, because he snapped, "Watch it!" and shoved Nick into the street.

"Sorry," Nick muttered and stepped back on the sidewalk.

"What'd you say?" the boy demanded. He and his friends came around and surrounded the two children and Sam.

"He said, 'Sorry,'" Sam said amiably. "No problem, right?"

"No problem for me," the boy snickered. "Big problems for you!" His friends laughed with him and Addie's throat went dry. "You might persuade me to forget about it, though." He took a menacing step toward Sam.

Sam held his ground and his voice was calm. "What do you need?"

Suddenly, another voice pierced the darkness. "Chill out, Donovan!"

Rico was trotting down the street, straightening his tie. When he reached the four boys he slapped four outstretched hands in a row.

"Hey, Don, hey, Carmen," he greeted two of the boys.

"What's with the monkey suit, Rico?" Carmen asked.

"Me and my friends are dinin' in style tonight," Rico answered.

"They with you?" Donovan's voice was incredulous.

"Hey, I'm hangin' with the rich and famous now," the boy grinned.

"Get what you can, Rico," Carmen laughed, and he and the others sauntered down the street and into the dark.

Rico fell into step next to Sam and the four of them walked in silence for more than a block. Finally Nick spoke.

"How did you happen to be there when we needed you?" he asked the boy.

"I heard Samson barkin' so I knew there were strangers in the neighborhood," Rico said. "When I saw who it was, I decided to follow you. I knew you wouldn't make it through the streets without trouble."

"Thanks," Addie said simply. "You're an answer to prayer."

They walked under a street light and Rico turned around to peer curiously into Addie's face. "You religious?"

Nick and Sam both grinned. Addie wasn't sure how to answer that question. She had been taught that being "religious" and being a Christian weren't necessarily the same thing. But she was pretty sure the semantics would be lost on Rico, so she simply nodded and said, "Kind of."

"You can't be 'kind of' Christian," Rico said, and Addie looked at him in surprise. "You either are or you ain't."

"Okay, I am," Addie replied.

"Thought so." Rico nodded. "Granny 'Zetti says you can always spot Christian folks. They got a gleam. Granny's got a gleam. So do you." Addie was touched by the boy's simple compliment and she didn't know what to say. Finally she asked, "Who's Granny 'Zetti?"

"My Grandma Marzetti," Rico explained. "She says prayers for me all the time."

He hesitated for a moment, then burst out, "I'm real sorry about your brush. But I don't think you want it now. One of the twins squeezed toothpaste all through the bristles. And I spent the money, so I can't pay you back, but—"

"You've already paid us back," Addie interrupted.

"That's right," Sam agreed. "Donovan and his friends might have been a real problem if you hadn't shown up."

"So we're even," Nick concluded.

They were back on Michigan Avenue and the Christmas lights lit up the night. Rico walked with them to the alley behind the center.

"Come in," Addie urged him. "I know Miss T. would like to meet—"

But Rico stopped her with a shake of his head. "Nah. We're even up. That's enough." He raised his hand in parting. "Bye."

He jammed both fists in his pockets and hurried back the way they had come. Soon his slight figure disappeared in the shadows.

CHAPTER 15

Welcome Surprises

Sam led the two children through the laundry to the narrow hall and back to the lobby. Miss T. and Amy still sat at the head table with Winston and some of the other dignitaries. A relieved look crossed Miss T.'s face when she saw the children approaching. Addie knew the two women had been worried about them, but all Miss T. said was, "How was your walk?"

"Informative," Sam replied and left it at that.

"Would you like to tour the display with us now?" Miss T. asked. "We have an hour or so before the program begins upstairs."

"Nah," Nick joked. "I've seen it all before."

Miss T. tried to glare at the boy, but Addie could tell she was amused. "Very funny, Mr. Brady. How about you, miss?"

"Of course," Addie smiled.

They spent the next hour walking through the museum's exhibit of Rinehart and Bryce memorabilia. The artifacts had been arranged according to the movie they were featured in. The backdrop for each display was a wall-sized photo of that movie's most memorable scene and many of the costumes were draped on life-size mannequins of Miss T. and Winston. Nick had great fun teasing Miss T. about the big pictures.

"Look at this one!" Nick hooted with laughter. "You need to pluck your eyebrows, Miss T." A young Tierny Bryce was scowling at Winston Rinehart and her dark brows were drawn together in a frown.

"You'd need to pluck yours too, if they were twelve inches across," the woman retorted.

Addie stopped in front of a mannequin wearing the dress from *The Lady Wore Red*. It was a gorgeous costume. Before Miss T. sold all her things months earlier, she allowed Addie to try the dress on and her father had taken a picture of her. No one else had seen the photo, but it was one of Addie's most treasured possessions.

Miss T. knew what Addie was thinking and she whispered in the girl's ear, "You looked much prettier in that dress than I ever did." Addie just grinned.

They made their way slowly around the room. Miss T. and Winston reminisced over each display and a small crowd followed them, listening to memories of bygone days. Finally the director of the museum approached them.

"I hate to interrupt, but the program upstairs is scheduled to begin in about ten minutes. I'll escort you to the banquet room whenever you're ready."

The banquet room was much smaller and more elegant than the lobby. The number of people attending the banquet had been cut by two-thirds. Addie decided if the people at the ribbon-cutting ceremony were Chicago's elite, the select group of people at the banquet must be Chicago's royalty.

There was a short film with the best clips from all the Rinehart and Bryce movies, narrated by the president of the screen actor's guild. Winston and Miss T. spoke briefly, sharing more memories and thanking the people of Chicago for their support.

It was a brief program and then the main meal began. There were tiny shrimp cocktail appetizers, some kind of wonderfully creamy soup, followed by a salad with big baskets of bread, and finally the main course of lobster and crab. In between each course, waiters brought them tiny little dishes of sherbert "to freshen the palate" and finger bowls and warm towels "to cleanse the hands."

Nick leaned over and whispered in Addie's ear. "The sherbert is great, but my fingers are going to get pruny if I have to wash them one more time."

Dessert was something chocolate and frothy and whipped, with sprinkles of hard chocolate on top. There wasn't much to it, but no one complained. They were too full.

"Roll me out of here," Nick finally groaned and Addie agreed. She felt like she'd been eating all day.

It was almost ten o'clock when the director of the museum thanked the guests of honor and wished everyone a Merry Christmas. It took another half-hour for the room to clear out while Miss T. and Winston signed more autographs.

"Let's get ready to leave," Amy suggested. "That will make it easier for Eunice to get away." The children agreed, and Sam went to find their coats. But when Addie put hers on, the scarf was missing.

"You had it when we got back from our walk," Nick said, "but it was hanging off one side of your coat. You probably dropped it in the laundry room downstairs."

"I'll go check," Addie said. She hurried down the winding stairs to the lobby. It was almost deserted, except for employees who were still cleaning up. She ducked through the swinging door and down the hall to the laundry room. Sure enough, her scarf was on the floor just by the exit to the alley. She picked it up and came back around the corner and almost ran into Joey.

"Whoops—you!" he exclaimed when he saw who it was. "You're a friend of Rico's, right?"

Addie nodded and the man continued. "You see Rico tonight?"

Addie nodded again. "We—"

"Good," Joey interrupted her. "You see Rico, you give him this." He pressed the brown paper package into her hand. "Tell him I can't use it. It's not laced. It's got to be laced or I can't use it. He knows where to find me." He disappeared around the corner before Addie could stop him.

"Thanks, kid." His voice echoed back from the alley and the metal door clanged shut behind him.

Addie stared in horror at the package she held, and her hands began to tremble. She looked all around to see if anyone was watching her, but she was alone in the laundry room.

She tore out into the hall, through the lobby, and took the stairs to the banquet room two at a time.

Her heels clicked loudly on the marble floor and everyone watched her run across the room.

"Addie, whatever is the matter?" Miss T. stopped the young girl and took her by the shoulders. "Catch your breath, dear. You look scared to death!"

"Joey gave me this," she gasped and held out the package. Nick stepped back as if it were a snake. "He said he can't use it if it's not laced!" She was trembling and her voice shook.

Sam quickly described the meeting Nick and Addie had witnessed between Rico and the man at the mall the previous day, and the conversation they had overheard between Rico and Joey earlier.

"So you think that package is some kind of drug," Miss T. said. Her voice sounded tight.

"I—I don't know what it is," Addie stuttered. "It's—it's—" Suddenly she flipped the package over in her hand. "It's really light," she finished in a puzzled voice.

Sam took the package from her and squeezed it. "Soft, too," he said. "I don't know what it is, but it's not drugs."

"Well, there's only one way to find out," Miss T. said. She took the package from Sam and slid one finger under a corner that had been taped down. The tape lifted easily and she opened the package. With a relieved smile, she pulled out a deep blue, hand-embroidered silk scarf.

The relief that flooded over Addie was so overwhelming she felt light-headed. Nick took a deep, shaky breath and began to laugh.

"That little scamp," Sam grinned and reached out to finger the soft, delicate material. "Wonder where he stole this from?"

"I think you may be judging Rico a little too harshly," Miss T. said. She turned the scarf over and showed them a small tag sown into the seam on the back side. The name "Marzetti" was embroidered there. "This is handmade. Probably by his mother."

"She must make these in her spare time and Rico sells them to the businessmen he meets when he hangs out at places like Jean-Luc's," Addie said.

"Why would a businessman want a silk scarf?" Nick asked.

"As a gift for his wife," Miss T. suggested.

"And I wouldn't be a bit surprised if she makes other things as well," Winston said. "She does beautiful work. There are boutiques all over town that would pay her well for a line of scarves like this one."

"I'm sorry we won't be seeing Rico again," Miss T. said. "I'd buy one of these from him."

Addie, Nick, and Sam exchanged guilty looks. "We could probably find him," Sam admitted and told the grown-ups the whole truth about their walk that night.

Amy was upset with her nephew. "That was not a wise thing to do," she chided him.

"I realized that when those punks came around the corner," he agreed: "I won't do it again."

"Good." Miss T. nodded her approval. "But since you did it this time, we ought to use your experience to our advantage. Could you find your way back to Rico's house?"

Sam nodded.

"Then let's pay the Marzettis a visit," Miss T. said.

They took the limo back to the hotel, but instead of going to their suite, they went out the back door to Sam's little Volkswagen. It was a tight squeeze with Winston in the car, but they managed and Sam pulled up to Marzetti Cleaners within a matter of minutes.

The store was dark and the door was locked, so Sam tossed a pebble at the second-story window. Rico's face appeared almost immediately.

"It's us, Rico," Nick shouted.

Rico opened the window. "You crazy?" he asked bluntly. "What's going on?"

"Can we come up?" Addie asked.

Mrs. Marzetti appeared behind Rico. The two of them talked briefly and Rico shouted back, "I'll be right there."

Soon the door to the store opened a crack and Rico peered out. His face was filled with fear. "Ma don't know nothing about—about nothing," he finished lamely and Miss T. hastened to quell the boy's fears.

"We're not here to get you in trouble, Rico," she said kindly. "I'd like to talk with your mother about her scarves." Miss T. held out the brown paper package and Rico grunted with surprise.

"Where'd you get that?" he asked suspiciously.

"We met Joey," Addie explained. "He wanted us to give it back to you. He can't use it unless it's laced."

Rico sniffed in disgust. "Joey ain't never satisfied," he muttered. He reached through the door and took the package from Miss T.

Nick began stomping his feet and clapping his hands together. "So can we come in or not?" he asked. "I'm freezing!"

Rico opened the door wide. "Sorry, dude," he grinned. "Come on in."

They all crowded into the tiny laundry and Rico surveyed the elegantly dressed group with a disbelieving shake of his head. "Ma's never gonna believe this!"

"A Future and a Hope"

It was after eleven o'clock and Rico's baby brother Mario was asleep in Addie's lap. Louie, one of the twins, was struggling valiantly to stay awake, but he was only five and soon he gave up the battle and fell asleep on the floor. The other twin, Vinnie, was still going strong and in a scuffle with Dominic, the seven-year-old, over possession of a matchbox car.

Rico stepped in and pulled the two apart. He solved the problem by plunking both boys down on opposite ends of a worn-out couch.

"Stay there," he ordered. He pocketed the car and the two little boys scowled at him but did as they were told.

Rico glanced anxiously in the kitchen, where his mother sat with Miss T. and Winston Rinehart. The wobbly kitchen table was a sea of color, filled with Gina Marzetti's handiwork. There were silk ties and pocket handkerchiefs for men, and embroidered scarves and silk vests for women.

"I still don't like it," he muttered and turned to Sam. "Why do we have to sell Ma's work at some bowtique?" he asked. "What kinda cut will they take? When I sell the tie, I bring home *all* the money," he said.

"You might not get as much money for each piece," Sam explained patiently, "but you'll sell a lot more so you'll make more money in the long run." Rico wasn't convinced and he continued to watch the scene in the kitchen with a worried frown.

Addie shifted Mario from one arm to the other and Vinnie toppled over on the couch, fast asleep. Rico picked him up and carried him into another room. When he returned he handed Dominic the car. Dominic took it with a satisfied smile and curled up on the couch and closed his eyes.

Chairs scraped across the linoleum floor in the kitchen and all the adults stood up. Winston came to the door of the living room and Mrs. Marzetti stood next to him.

"Mr. Rinehart is going with me tomorrow to a boutique his friend owns down on Michigan Avenue," she told Rico. "He thinks I can sell my work for a good price. They might even commission me to do more."

"I been sellin' your work, Ma," Rico said in a low voice.

"And you'll have to help even more now," Winston told the boy.

"How?" Rico wanted to know.

"All your regular customers will have to know where they can find your mother's work once it's in stores," Winston informed him. "And you must continue to tell the business people you meet about your mother's talent. Word-of-mouth advertising is always the best," he said. "And I've never seen you at a loss for words!"

Mrs. Marzetti laughed and Rico grinned reluctantly. The woman pulled her son close. "You've got good friends, Rico," she murmured.

"They've got Granny 'Zetti's gleam," he agreed.

While the adults finished talking, Addie laid little Mario on the couch next to Dominic, then pulled Rico to one side. "Can we buy some things tonight?" she asked.

Rico's face brightened considerably. "What do you need?" he said in his best salesman's voice.

Addie chose a silk tie for her father. She and Nick pooled their money and bought Miss T. and Amy each a scarf similar to the one Miss T. had admired earlier. When they were finished, Rico had every penny they had, but neither of them cared.

They said goodbye to their new friends after midnight. The ride home was a quiet one. Sam navigated his way through the Chicago streets with ease. Soon they were back at Jean-Luc's and Marcia was opening the steel door to the service entrance.

"What pretty scarves!" she exclaimed when she saw Miss T.'s and Amy's gifts.

Miss T. smiled. "Rico can tell you all about them," she said.

"Rico?"

Everyone nodded, but no one had the energy to explain.

"Tell me in the morning," Marcia laughed. "You all look like you're going to fall asleep on your feet!"

Winston bid everyone good night at the elevator and went to his own suite on the first floor. The elevator door "ponged" open and they all stepped in.

Addie leaned against the wall and closed her eyes. There was a smile on her face and Miss T. noticed.

"Are you satisfied, miss?" the elderly woman asked.

Addie simply nodded. She had wanted so desperately to help Rico, and she thanked God right there for giving them the chance to see Gina Marzetti's work. She knew the Lord would work out the details at the boutique.

And Addie was convinced there was a "future and a hope" for Rico. After all, he had a grandma who gleamed.

Don't Miss Any of Addie McCormick's Exciting Adventures!

Addie McCormick and the Stranger in the Attic

A vanishing visitor and secrets from the past... can Addie and Nick put the puzzle together before something terrible happens to their friend Miss T.?

Addie McCormick and the Mystery of the Missing Scrapbook

A missing scrapbook, mysterious paintings, and an old letter lead Nick, Addie, and Brian on a heartstopping chase. Are they in over their heads this time?

Addie McCormick and the Stolen Statue

A movie star has been kidnapped and Miss T.'s statue has disappeared! Facing their toughest mystery yet, Addie, Nick, and Brian have all the clues... but can they put them together before it's too late?

Addie McCormick and the Chicago Surprise

When things start disappearing from their hotel room in Chicago, Addie and Nick are determined to solve the mystery. But what they discover about the thief is much more than they bargained for!

Other Good Harvest House Reading

THE CHRISTA CHRONICLES
by *Mark Littleton*

Secrets of Moonlight Mountain

When an unexpected blizzard traps Crista on Moonlight Mountain with a young couple in need of a doctor, Crista must brave the storm and the dark to get her physician father. An exciting story of friendship and courage that draws Crista and her dad together.

Winter Thunder

A sudden change in Crista's new friend, Jeff, and the odd circumstances surrounding Mrs. Oldham's broken windows all point to Jeff as the culprit in the recent vandalism around the lake. Jeff's mysterious past resolves itself through a dramatic rescue and the love of newfound friends.

The Great Bible Adventure
by *Sandy Silverthorne*

This creative 32-page book is designed with 14 best-loved Bible stories set into full double-page illustrations. Every story has several different objects highlighted for the kids to find in the big picture. Silverthorne's zany sense of humor drives him to add extra surprises that will have children coming back to see if they've missed anything!